Attention: Courag[...] personnel
From: U.S. Coast Guard

This is to notify all emergency personnel that a helicopter has been reported missing over Courage Bay near S-hamala Island. The helicopter is piloted by Dan Egan, fire chief of Jefferson Avenue Firehouse. Also on board is Dr. Natalie Giroux, a staff member of Courage Bay Hospital. The two were returning to the local airport after a successful emergency airlift of a male heart-attack victim from the mudslide on Courage Bay mountain. Reports indicate the fire chief's dog is also in the copter.

Final contact with air traffic control was made shortly after the helicopter took off from the hospital helipad late this afternoon. All reports indicate that the pilot changed course to avoid the approaching storm. Further attempts by air traffic control to contact Chief Egan have been unsuccessful, suggesting radio failure or a forced landing. Gale-force winds are reported in the bay area, along with twenty-foot swells. A large- and small-craft warning has been issued for the surrounding waters. All flights are grounded in and out of Courage Bay airport, and coast guard personnel were evacuated from S-hamala Island to the mainland earlier this afternoon. Given the current conditions, any search-and-rescue missions are on hold until further notice. Updates will be issued on an hourly basis.

TORI CARRINGTON

Nationally bestselling, multi-award-winning husband-and-wife duo Lori and Tony Karayianni are the power behind the pen name Tori Carrington. With more than twenty-five novels to their credit, they approach every new book with the same awe and enthusiasm as their first. Along with their two adult sons, Tony Jr. and Tim, they call Toledo, Ohio, home base, but travel to Tony's hometown of Athens, Greece, as often as they can. To learn more about this prolific couple, visit their Web site at www.toricarrington.com.

CODE RED

TORI CARRINGTON

TOTAL EXPOSURE

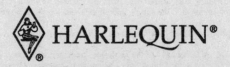

HARLEQUIN®

TORONTO • NEW YORK • LONDON
AMSTERDAM • PARIS • SYDNEY • HAMBURG
STOCKHOLM • ATHENS • TOKYO • MILAN • MADRID
PRAGUE • WARSAW • BUDAPEST • AUCKLAND

HARLEQUIN BOOKS
225 Duncan Mill Road, Don Mills,
Ontario, Canada M3B 3K9

ISBN 0-373-61287-7

TOTAL EXPOSURE

Copyright © 2004 by Harlequin Books S.A.

Tori Carrington is acknowledged as the author of this work

www.eHarlequin.com

Printed in U.S.A.

Dear Reader,

As steadfast fans of Harlequin's continuity series, we were thrilled when we were invited to contribute to the CODE RED series. Actually, contribute is the wrong word, because, as we quickly discovered, these series are team endeavors in which every member plays an important role—from editor down to the author of the last title—making for a unique reading and writing experience we'll treasure always.

In *Total Exposure,* our hunky hero, Fire Chief Dan Egan, is every bit the alpha male with a chip on his shoulder that beautiful burn specialist Natalie Giroux only aggravates. Dan's wounds run far deeper than the burn he suffered three months earlier in a warehouse explosion. But when he's stranded with Natalie on a deserted island during one of the worst storms in Courage Bay's history, does this man of action have the courage to let the lady doc heal all of his wounds so they might forge a future together?

We hope you enjoy Dan and Natalie's rocky journey to happily-ever-after! We'd love to hear from you. Write us at P.O. Box 12271, Toledo, Ohio 43612 or e-mail us at toricarrington@aol.com. And make sure you visit our Web site at www.toricarrington.com for info on coming attractions and to enter our latest online drawings.

Here's wishing you love, romance and heartfelt reading!

Lori and Tony Karayianni
Aka Tori Carrington

We warmly dedicate this book to the extraordinary Marsha Zinberg and her phenomenal support team, including Alethea Spiridon, Sasha Bogin and Margaret Learn for helping us "expose" another facet of ourselves as writers and human beings. Thank you!

CHAPTER ONE

In Dr. Natalie Giroux's experience, there were days that were great, others that were so-so and a handful of additional ones she'd prefer to erase from the record books altogether. Unfortunately, this cold, rainy Friday in November fell solidly into the last category. Not so much because of the threatening storm system that had been parked over Courage Bay, California, for the past couple of days. It was, after all, the rainy season, and, well, rain was to be expected. Her sluggishness didn't stem from the long, hard week she'd just gone through as Courage Bay Hospital's burn specialist, treating a wide variety of injuries she somehow never got quite used to seeing. Nor could her mood be blamed on nothing going according to plan, or the fact she'd been misplacing things all day.

No. The source of her melancholy was far more personal and went much deeper than such simple matters. And as a result, the dark monster was much more difficult to battle.

Natalie blinked her examining room back into focus, then gently tousled the head of a four-year-old burn patient in for a follow-up appointment.

"That's it," she said, helping the girl down from the table. "We're all done. Now, that wasn't so difficult, was it?"

She trailed the girl and her mother into the reception area. Little Jenny Barnard was recovering nicely. Natalie wished she could say that about all of her patients. She held up three different flavored suckers. Jenny took the yellow, lemon-flavored one.

"Now, do you remember everything I told you?" Natalie asked the four-year-old. "You've got to drink lots of juice and let your mom change your bandages when she says it's time." The superficial dermal burn on the right side of Jenny's face was the result of an unfortunate accident involving a pot of boiling spaghetti, a cat and the young girl a week ago. But the injury was not what Natalie focused on now that the examination was over. All she saw was Jenny's vibrant spirit.

"I will, Dr. Natalie."

Natalie smiled and crossed her arms over the girl's chart, hugging it to her, as she watched mother and daughter walk down the hall of the hospital. When they were out of sight, she glanced at her watch, trying to ignore the large numbers of the date at the left. She made a few notes on the chart, then slid it into the slot outside the examining room door for her assistant to pick up.

Today would have been her first wedding anniversary.

The thought snagged her attention, nearly causing the next chart she drew out to drop from her numb fingers.

She swallowed hard, seeking the solace she usually found in her work.

It wasn't so much the fact that she and Charles would have celebrated their first year of marriage today. She'd been mentally preparing herself for that milestone over the past month. What made her heart ache was that the week before their wedding day, she'd lost Charles. Not to another woman. Not to a case of cold feet. No, the loss was even more decisive. Natalie had lost him to heart disease. Permanently.

She cleared her throat and flipped open the chart in her hands, grateful to be so busy. During the past year, the hospital and her patients were all that had stood between her and emotional collapse.

But nothing seemed capable of helping her through today.

Her gaze fell on the name at the top of the chart and she sighed, glancing around the waiting area without much hope of finding who she was looking for.

"He didn't show," her assistant, Manuela, said from her desk on the other side of the reception area. "Again."

"What appointment is this?" Natalie asked. "His fourth?"

"Fifth."

Natalie skimmed the contents of the chart. Fire Chief Dan Egan might be everything and more than his stellar reputation suggested when it came to his work, but keeping his appointments with her seemed to rank low on his list of priorities.

She leaned against the doorjamb, then turned the page of the file, although she really didn't need to. She already knew what it would tell her. Namely that the fire chief had suffered a contact burn to his side in the warehouse explosion three months ago. The severe blistering and her inability to judge the depth of the wound had required a follow-up appointment for her to better evaluate the injury and make assessments for additional treatment. Only the handsome fire chief had canceled that appointment. And the next one he'd made for a week after that. Until she stood right where she was now—essentially without the information she needed in order to close the file.

"Should I call and reschedule?" Manuela asked, interrupting her thoughts.

"Hmm? Oh." She flipped the chart closed. "No."

"Are you going to leave the file open?"

Natalie stared over the young woman's shoulder to the wall and the seascapes hanging there. But she didn't see the warm pastel colors depicting what was visible through any window looking over Courage Bay. Instead her mind conjured up an image of Charles right before his death. A staff psychologist with the hospital, Charles had refused to follow up on symptoms that in retrospect had foreshadowed the fatal heart attack that took his life.

"Are you all right, Natalie?" Manuela asked quietly.

Natalie's chest felt cramped and congested. Only she wasn't coming down with a virus. At least not one that could be treated. Rather, it was raw emotion that choked off her breath and made her feel sick to her stomach.

Nothing she had said had made a difference with Charles. And there was no reason to believe that she'd have any more pull when it came to Dan Egan.

She shook her head. "It's been three months since the warehouse incident. I'm going to close the file."

The phone on Manuela's desk rang as Natalie glanced at her watch again. Three-thirty. Since her last appointment for the day was a no-show, she had some unexpected time on her hands.

The last thing she wanted.

"Natalie?"

She looked at Manuela.

"It's Debra Egan for you. Shall I take a message?"

Debra Egan. Dan Egan's daughter. Natalie often forgot that little detail because her connection to them took different forms. While Dan was her no-show patient, Debra led an exercise class at a local gym. A class Natalie took whenever she could fit it into her busy schedule.

Maybe she could go over there now. Work off some of the energy burning her from the inside out.

She motioned down the corridor. "I'll take the call in my office. Thanks, Manuela."

Leaving her door open, she put Dan's chart on her narrow desk, sat down and plucked up the telephone receiver.

She'd barely said hello before Debra asked, "Is he there?"

Natalie reached for the pile of folders in her in box. "If you're referring to your father, no. Unless he's running late, he stood me up again." She shuffled through the files until she located the one she was looking for, on a grease-fire patient.

"So Nate lied to me…again." Debra sighed. "I just called the station and he told me Dad was at the hospital."

"Maybe he is here somewhere, just not with me."

Silence reigned as Natalie reviewed the details on a patient who needed her help much more than the city's stubborn fire chief. After a few moments, she realized Debra had still not replied. "Is everything all right, Deb?"

"I'm sorry. I didn't mean to zone out on you, Natalie. It's just that…well, I've been taking on double classes here. And when I'm not working—heck, even when I am—I'm worrying about Dad. Just the other day I caught him wincing when he reached to pick up something. That burn is bothering him, but he won't own up to it."

"I can't do anything about it if he won't let me," Natalie said quietly.

"I know. I was just thinking, you know, if you wouldn't mind too much, you could go over to the station yourself to check him out."

Natalie briefly closed her eyes. While she didn't mind making the occasional house call, the thought of chasing Dan Egan around, trying to get a look at him without his shirt on, struck her as ridiculous.

"I mean, you were scheduled to see him right now, anyway, weren't you? The fire station is only a couple blocks away from the hospital…."

Natalie propped her elbow on her desk. "Deb, I…"

"Please, Natalie. I'm really worried. I mean, after what happened with Mom…"

There was a plaintive tone in the nineteen-year-old's voice. Sometimes Natalie found it hard to remember that Debra was almost twenty years younger than she was. But at times like these, when she was reminded that Dan Egan's wife had died of breast cancer only two short years ago, she realized how young and still hurt Debra was.

"I'll throw in a couple free exercise sessions," the young woman said, her voice overly bright.

Natalie took a deep breath and told herself if she did this, she wouldn't be doing it for Dan Egan, but as a favor to his daughter.

"Okay," she said, smiling at the enormous sigh of relief filling her ear. "I'll go to the station. But I can't promise anything, Deb. I mean, if he doesn't want me to examine him, I can't exactly cut his shirt off him."

The idea of peeling away Dan Egan's shirt to reveal his muscular torso sent a mild shiver running through her—one unfamiliar and ultimately unwelcome.

"Oh, thank you, Natalie! You don't know how much this means to me."

"I think I do, Deb," she said softly. "That's why I'm doing it."

"I'm going to call the station right now and tell him you're coming."

Natalie opened her mouth to object, but the line was already disconnected.

She slowly hung up. Odds were that if Dan Egan knew she was coming, he'd run full tilt in the opposite direction.

FIRE CHIEF DAN EGAN loved his job, but like most professions, there were aspects he hated with a passion. And paperwork ranked right up near the top.

He pulled together the rotation schedules scattered across his desk and started putting them in order by week. Too bad Courage Bay's budget didn't allow for a full-time office manager. He could really use one. Especially now, so close to the holidays. It wasn't hard to understand why everyone wanted Thanksgiving off. But it was up to him and his two captains to decide who would actually get their request. While seniority played a role, Dan also had to consider who had worked the last holiday, and other variables.

This was all stuff he'd prefer not to have to think about. He'd much rather be out on a run somewhere instead of stuck in his office trying to make heads or tails out of Captain Joe Ripani's indecipherable chicken scratches. Dan turned a page one way, then another, trying to make out a notation. At last he gave up and tossed the paper aside. The white sheet drifted on the air and started sailing over the side of his desk toward the wastebasket. He made a move to catch it, pulling the three-month-old burn on his side and causing pain to shoot up his back and down his arm.

"Damn."

Spike, a twelve-year-old Dalmatian and his constant companion nowadays, lay sprawled in front of the door. At the sound of Dan's voice, he lifted his head and gave a quiet bark.

Dan grimaced at him. "I bet you know exactly how I feel, don't you, boy?" He gingerly leaned back in his chair. "Too old to do any of the fun stuff, too young not to want to do it."

While Spike hadn't been the official fire dog for some years now due to age, his role at the station had been called into question by the new firehouse mascot, Salvage, a black Lab that truckie Shannon O'Shea had rescued from a warehouse fire. A second fire at the same warehouse was responsible for Dan's burn.

Yes, Dan had found out exactly how it felt to be phased out—or rather, "promoted"—when he made fire chief a year ago, leaving his days of hands-on action well behind him.

The small, recessed speaker in the ceiling broadcast an incoming phone call to the station's general line. Dan purposely ignored it, because for all intents and purposes he wasn't there. He was supposed to be at the hospital getting a checkup from that frustratingly beautiful Dr. Natalie Giroux. An appointment he had no intention of keeping.

He caught himself lightly rubbing the wound in question, then put both hands firmly on his desk as Spike laid his head back down on top of his paws.

"Chief? Call's for you." Nate Kellison's voice sounded over the speaker. Nate was a paramedic on Squad Two.

Cursing under his breath, Dan leaned back in his chair to yell out the open door. "I'm not here."

"She's not buying it," came the answer.

Dan snatched the receiver from its cradle on his desk. "Egan."

"I knew I'd get you if I threatened Nate with the rotation from hell." His daughter's voice filtered into his ear. "But my question is, why are you there instead of at the hospital like you're supposed to be?"

"Something came up."

"Right. Just like something's come up the past four times you were scheduled to meet with Natalie."

The mention of the lady doc's name made Dan's stomach tighten.

He told himself the thought of her poking and prodding at him was behind the physical response. If the memory of her mocha-colored eyes above her surgical mask when he'd finally come to in the hospital three months ago had anything to do with his reaction, well, he wasn't about to own up to it.

Mocha? Where in the hell had that description come from? He rubbed his forehead with his finger and thumb. Must be Tim and all that fancy cappuccino stuff he made whenever he was on duty. Dr. Natalie Giroux's eyes were brown. Nothing more, nothing less.

And Dan hated hospitals. Nothing more, nothing less.

There weren't very many things capable of putting the fear of God into Dan Egan. He'd joined the Courage Bay Fire Department after completing six years of active military service as a helicopter pilot flying emergency missions in war-torn areas of the world. He'd done it all—firefighter, haz-mat specialist, smoke jumper, helicopter pilot, captain. When Patrick O'Shea became mayor last year, freeing up the top position in the fire department, Dan had moved up to chief. Yes, he'd pretty much faced every intimidating situation that there was to face.

But hospitals…

He cursed under his breath.

"I told you," he said to his daughter, "and I'm going to keep telling you until you get it through that thick head of yours—I'm fine. I don't need to go to the doctor for a checkup."

"And I told you," Debra countered without missing a beat, "and I'm going to keep telling you until you get it through that thick head of yours, it's just a follow-up. If it's true you're fine, then what better way to shut me up than by letting Natalie take a look?"

There went that stomach-tightening thing again.

Next to hospitals, Burn Specialist Natalie Giroux was second on his most-hated list. Well, maybe not most-hated. But definitely a woman to avoid. While her eyes were soft and intriguing, her take-charge manner rubbed him the wrong way. Although he didn't consider himself sexist—he was the first to admit the two female firefighters at the station more than pulled their own weight— Natalie…well, Natalie seemed to go that one inch too far.

Pushy. That's what he'd like to think his late wife would have called her. A pushy woman.

"Are you done?" he asked his nineteen-going-on-forty-year-old daughter. "Because if you are, there are some important things I could be doing."

"If you're not on a run, then it's not important," she countered. "Anyway, I just called to make sure you're there. I convinced Natalie to stop by and conduct her examination."

"Here?" he repeated. "Here, as in the station?"

"Yes. And you'd better be nice to her."

Nice to her, hell. He wasn't going to be there.

"Deb, I've got to go."

"Call me—"

Dan didn't hear the rest because he was in the process of hanging up.

If Dr. Natalie Giroux was on her way to the station, that meant he had to be on his way out.

He pushed to his feet, wincing again as the scar tissue pulled tight. He grabbed his jacket, then headed for the door. Spike lumbered to his feet, the chain collar around his neck clinking as he wagged his tail and followed.

Dan hurried down the hall toward the bays at the front of the station, calling out as he went. "Nate? I'm out of here. If you need anything, I'll be—"

The words stopped dead in his throat as he literally bumped into the woman he was trying to avoid, along with her unsettling mocha-brown eyes.

Dr. Natalie Giroux blocked his path, looking none too happy as rain ran in rivulets from the umbrella she held.

"You'll be where?" she asked.

CHAPTER TWO

NATALIE HELD HER GROUND as she faced off with an obviously shocked and disappointed Dan Egan in the open bay of the fire station. She had little doubt he'd been trying to ditch her. The instant Debra had said she'd be calling her father, Natalie had hurried to the station, determined to get this over with once and for all. Close the file on the sexy and infuriating Dan Egan, who could easily serve as the poster boy for stubborn men worldwide.

She gazed into his light blue eyes and found herself swallowing hard to rid her mouth of the moisture that had instantly collected there. She'd forgotten how...big he was. And that was saying a lot, because at five-seven, she didn't exactly rank on the short side. But Dan...Dan easily topped six-three. Six feet three inches of hard, solid, attractive male.

Of hard, mulish, injured male, she reminded herself.

"I, um," Dan mumbled, squinting at her against a shaft of late afternoon sunlight that had suddenly speared through the thick, heavy storm clouds blanketing the Courage Bay area. "I have to run some errands."

"Good thing you didn't say you had an appointment." Natalie couldn't help a wry smile, although she felt cold and wet, and her day had taken an even steeper nosedive when she'd agreed to this particular call.

He absently scratched the back of his neck near the neat line of his dark brown hair. "Did we have an appointment today?"

A clacking sound caught Natalie's attention, and she gasped as something brushed against her bare knee. She looked down at the white dog with huge black spots all over him. "Don't tell me," she said. "This must be Spot."

Dan slid his fingers into the dog's chain-link collar and pulled him back. "Actually, it's Spike."

Natalie blinked at him.

Dan grinned. "His grandfather was Spot."

"Ah," she said, not quite sure how to react to the information or the warm grin that came along with it. She tried to look over Dan's shoulder, then glanced around him instead at the mammoth red ladder truck glistening in the shaft of light. A moment later the light disappeared and dark gloom settled in once again, a steady rain pelting the station roof.

"Looks like this storm's not going anywhere for a while."

Natalie glanced at the ominous purple clouds. Were they really talking about the weather? It had rained for the past seven days straight. "It *is* the rainy season in Southern Cal."

He seemed to consider her. "That it is."

"Where do you want to do this?" Natalie asked.

Dan's eyes widened slightly. "Do what?"

"If you're in that much of a rush, we could do it right here."

"Here?"

"The examination." She tightened her fingers around the black bag she held along with her umbrella, not comfortable with the other possibilities that came to mind. Why did she feel so drawn to this man, reading sexual innuendo into a simple comment?

But Dan was too much like Charles—so not what she wanted or needed right now. Nor anytime in the foreseeable future.

"Oh." He looked around, as if realizing where they were for the first time. "We could go to my office."

"That'll work."

He started walking away, then glanced over his shoulder. "Will this take long?"

"Depends."

He slowed his steps, nearly causing her to plow into him. "On what?"

Natalie tried not to look at the way the denim of his jeans hugged his backside. "Have you had any problems since the injury? I mean, aside from the normal healing process?"

He shook his head. "No problems."

"No soreness, tightness, sharp pains?"

He seemed to hesitate for a moment. "Nope. None of that."

"Well, then, this shouldn't take any time at all," Natalie said, hoping fervently that was the case. She didn't like the way she felt when she was around Dan Egan. His presence…did things to her. Short-circuited her mental wiring. Kicked up her heartbeat. Reminded her that she was a woman who hadn't been with a man in a long time.

Today would have been your wedding anniversary, a small voice whispered to her.

Charles is gone, another said.

"Are you okay?"

They had stopped outside an office Natalie guessed was his. "That's funny," she said with a small smile. "I thought I was supposed to be the one asking that question."

His gaze skimmed over her face, but he didn't say anything.

Once again Natalie felt that heightened awareness of Dan as a man. She put her bag down on the cluttered desktop and opened it up. "Take off your jacket and shirt," she said in her most professional tone.

"Pardon me?"

His voice held a slight Southern drawl. Natalie had forgotten that Dan hailed from Turning Point, Texas. And though a long time had passed since he'd actually lived there, his voice, his mannerisms, and yes, even his charm, were decidedly Texan.

"I can't examine you through your clothes, Dan," she said quietly.

"Oh."

He obviously wasn't looking forward to this any more than she was. Just being near him again made Natalie remember how affected she'd been by him three months ago. When he was brought in to the emergency room, unconscious, after the warehouse explosion, she'd noticed how strikingly handsome he was. How powerful looking. When she'd peeled back the sheet to examine the blistered skin on his side, he'd blinked open those pale blue eyes, and she'd felt the shock of connection.

Immediately she'd repressed her response and focused on the job she had to do. But she hadn't forgotten.....

"Dan, I really need you to—"

"Okay—"

An earsplitting alarm went off and at the same time the cadence of the heavily falling rain intensified against the station roof.

Spike barked and wove circles around their legs even as Dan straightened his jacket and headed through the open doorway without so much as an explanation or apologetic glance.

Natalie gathered her bag and umbrella and followed after him, not about to be put off again. If she had to conduct this examination while he was putting out a fire, by God, she was going to do it.

DAN CLIMBED BEHIND the wheel of his service Jeep, allowed Spike to climb up over him and into the back seat, then switched on the siren. He was about to put the vehicle into gear when the passenger door opened and Natalie slid in next to him.

His gaze fell on the way her skirt hiked up from the climb, revealing her slender legs. She seemed to realize what he was looking at and immediately remedied the situation, tugging her hem down to cover her knees.

Ladder truck #1 blew its horn some twenty feet away as it pulled out of the bay and onto the street, siren blaring, redirecting Dan's attention.

"Where do you think you're going?" he demanded of Natalie, a hairbreadth away from reaching over her to open the door and shove the lady doc out.

"With you, of course." She crossed her arms in a maddening way that emphasized the gentle curves beneath her rain slicker and blouse. "I'm going to close the case on you today, no matter what it takes."

Dan stared at her. There weren't very many people who could stand up to his scowl, and he focused it on Natalie full force.

To her credit—or stupidity—she didn't even blink. Instead, her delicate chin came up a little higher and those mocha eyes held a challenge he'd previously seen in fellow combatants' eyes.

Mocha? He shoved the Jeep into gear before realizing he'd decided to do so. Her eyes were brown. Nothing more. Nothing less.

Spike's head poked between the seats. He whined softly, looking first at Dan, then at Natalie.

"I know what you mean, buddy," Dan said between clenched teeth. "I know what you mean."

NATALIE HAD LISTENED as Dan spoke on his radio to dispatch during the ride to the site, but had understood little of the codes and commands. She had witnessed many gut-wrenching scenes while on duty at the hospital's burn unit, and inwardly prepared herself now for the worst. Dan pulled to a stop behind the ladder truck, the rain pounding on the windshield so heavily she only had a split second to see what lay outside before sheets of water again blocked her view.

"What…what's going on?" she asked, the sound of her heartbeat loud in her ears.

"Mudslide," Dan said, bounding from the car, his dog following after him. Natalie craned her neck to watch him, noticing the way both dog and master stood in the onslaught, neither seeming aware of the rain as they took in the situation.

Natalie fastened her rain slicker tightly, then grabbed her umbrella. The instant she opened the door she was hit by a wall of rain and wind that stole her breath from her. She sputtered, tightly gripping the molding of the door as she climbed out, fighting to hold on to the umbrella she was trying to open.

"Stay in the car!" Dan shouted, striding purposely toward the spot where his men were gathering their gear.

Natalie squinted after him as she pulled the umbrella as close to her head as she could. Stay in the car? What did he think she was, some kind of unruly child? She was a physician used to responding to emergency situations. Okay, so they usually involved burn victims who had already been transported to the hospital. But she wasn't stupid. She started to step around the ladder truck, her foot plopping into a particularly nasty puddle with spongy mud beneath. Maybe she'd have to be a little more careful, but she wasn't stupid.

Spike's bark drew her closer to the front of the truck. Exercising caution, she stepped clear of the vehicle, then stopped dead in her tracks. She hadn't realized where they were until that very moment. Before her towered Courage Bay Mountain, looking like an ominous monster in the dim purple light. The city of Courage Bay spread out along a ten-mile stretch of clean, white-sand beaches bordering the Pacific Ocean north of Los Angeles. Steep, forested mountains surrounded the crescent of lush coastal land. But after a particularly brutal drought last summer, the mountains were vulnerable to mudslides in this year's rainy season.

Wealthier residents of the city had built expensive homes that jutted out of the side of Courage Bay Mountain facing the bay—on a steep slope the rain had turned into an unstable mound of mud. Natalie shielded her eyes and watched as a house halfway up the hill slid a couple feet sideways, its front pilings collapsing under the shifting weight.

Oh, God.

That something so seemingly solid could be easily swept off its foundations gave her pause.

"Over there!" one of Dan's men shouted, indicating a man waving frantically at them from where he stood near the side of his house. An ominous crack sounded. Natalie watched the man slip and slide away from the structure toward a stand of trees where a woman and two young kids huddled.

It all looked so…overwhelming. So hopeless. How could the firefighters possibly reach them? There was no way they could get up there. And how would the family get down? Given the steady pounding of the rain and the already treacherous slopes, the situation could only get worse.

"Go!"

Natalie blinked and turned her head to find Dan shouting the order to four men wearing rappelling gear. Two by two, connected together by ropes, they headed for the foot of the mountain and began climbing the sturdiest-looking part of the hill.

"Team south, go!" Dan shouted again, and four more men headed down the road to the other side of the slide, carefully maneuvering their way through mud and debris flowing over the two-lane coastal highway toward the sea.

Standing pole still, strangely immune to the rain pelting her despite her slicker and umbrella, Natalie stared at the bear of a man she'd been trying to bully into letting her examine him such a short time ago. He looked so powerful, so capable. And his mere presence made the situation seem less desperate. More than a natural disaster, the mudslide was a challenge to be met. A job to be done. And she sensed that Dan Egan was exactly the man to do it.

Spike barked. Natalie jumped, surprised to find the dalmatian standing next to her. She glanced over to see Dan looking her way. Their gazes met across the twenty-foot expanse, neither of them blinking despite the rain streaming down their faces. As if they were joined in some odd, reassuring way.

One of Dan's men held out something for him to look at, forcing him to break eye contact. Natalie let go of the breath she was holding, then turned her head and briefly closed her eyes.

Please, she prayed, *please don't let me fall for this man....*

TWENTY MINUTES LATER the rain began to let up a bit, though not enough to make a significant difference. Dan stared up at the angry winter sky, asking for any kind of break he could get. While the lessening rain had little impact on the severity of the situation, it did create a better working environment for his men.

He scanned the mountainside, searching for the two rescue squads. The north team had already anchored a lead rope and was harnessing up the family of four to come down one by one. The south team was having a harder time finding a solid foothold from which to operate.

The civil engineer he'd ordered dispatch to contact held out the plastic-covered schematic of the houses on the hill. Of the more than a dozen homes, two were almost completely swallowed by the cascading mud, either buried outright or in pieces, and four more were about to give way. The bridge spanning the pass had been washed out, making those houses inaccessible. The rescue team had to move quickly.

He pulled his two-way to his mouth. "South team, status report."

"Surface unstable. No foothold, sir. Repeat, we can't get a foothold. Over."

Dan eyed the terrain around the team. "Go fifteen paces southeast, Captain, and see if you can get a lock on the rock there by the trees."

"Roger that."

He watched the leader of the south team secure his radio, then point out the route to his men. On the other side, the stranded mother was cautiously sliding down the taut rope, a firefighter from the north team at her back to ease the way.

Dan caught himself rubbing the back of his damp neck, awareness crawling over his skin. While the doc hadn't stayed in the car as he'd asked, she had stayed out of the way, staring at the mudslide, her eyes wide, looking particularly vulnerable.

Now that was a word he wouldn't have used to describe Natalie Giroux only an hour ago. As he recalled, pushy was the adjective he'd chosen. She stood at the foot of the hill, appearing to want to do something, but aware that she wasn't qualified.

He grudgingly gave her credit. He knew what it was like to be stuck on the sidelines. At forty-five, he'd had to trade an active role for that of coordinator. But the urge to rush into the fray was something he wasn't good at quelling. Not yet. And, he was coming to fear, not ever. As it was, he now fisted and unfisted his hands, his pulse pounding with the impulse to climb up the shifting mountainside and help those in need.

"Doesn't look good."

Dan turned to address the man at his side. K-9 Patrol Officer Cole Winslow's rain gear wasn't much protection against the storm blasting them, but he seemed oblivious to it. He held the lead to Braveheart, his black-and-tan German shepherd.

"What brings you out to this neck of the woods?" Dan asked after he directed team members on the ground to help the rescued mother from her harness and to safety.

"Actually, I was already here. You've heard about the series of break-ins in the area recently? Well, the prowler was spotted in one of the houses. Braveheart and I were called in to track his scent."

"Which house?"

Cole nodded toward the northeast and a house that a river of mud was claiming even as they watched. "Dylan Deeb's place. You know, that producer who was brought up on sexual assault charges six months ago?"

Dan was familiar with the case. Deeb was a slimebag with a capital *S*. He was accused of coercing underage actresses into having sex with him in exchange for parts in his movies. The charges were dropped when the actresses refused to testify against him. Likely Deeb had convinced them their careers would do better with him on this side of prison bars.

"You get the prowler?" Dan asked.

The officer shook his head. "Lost his scent at the marina. A small boat was reported stolen an hour ago, so my guess is he borrowed it and headed out onto the bay."

Glancing at the churning waters in the distance, Dan wondered if the prowler would have been better off facing Cole and prison than the storm-tossed sea.

A car raced up behind him and ground to a screeching stop on the wet asphalt. It had obviously passed the barriers his men had placed a quarter of a mile up the road. Like a river of brown lava, the debris path had sheared the highway in two, blocking traffic on both sides. He glanced at the older model vehicle and the young blond woman who stumbled out of it. She stared at the mountain in horror. A resident? Possibly. He motioned toward a junior firefighter to stop her from advancing, then concentrated on controlling his own overactive adrenaline.

BRITTNEY MACKENZIE COULDN'T believe her eyes. She stumbled forward, staring at the disintegrating mountain in front of her. She'd been there only an hour before and everything had been fine. Now the road she had taken to drive up to film producer Dylan

Deeb's house was indistinguishable from the rest of the oozing mud eating the highway.

Fine? Had she really just used the word *fine* to describe what had happened in Dylan Deeb's house only sixty minutes ago?

"Miss, I'm afraid I'm going to have to ask you to step back."

She blinked unseeingly into the face of a young firefighter in yellow waterproof overalls and black boots. "What… How…" The words came out of her mouth but she couldn't seem to form a coherent sentence as she desperately sought out the producer's house. Her heart beat an uneven rhythm in her chest.

It's gone.

Along with any chance of her ever becoming a working actress.

Remorse, shame and fear rose up in her throat, choking her.

"Whoa, easy there," she heard the firefighter say right before her legs went out from under her.

When she became aware of the world around her again, what could have been minutes or hours later, she was blinking into the face of a pretty woman who reminded her of her mother.

"Can you hear me?" the woman asked, waving a penlight in front of her eyes.

Brittney squeezed them shut against the intrusive light. "I can hear you."

"How many fingers am I holding up?"

Brittney squinted. "Three."

She realized then that she was lying across the front seat of her own car.

"Do you live here? Is there someone I can call? When's the last time you had anything to eat?"

Eat?

Brittney struggled to a sitting position. "I'm fine. Really, I am." She pulled her shaking legs inside the car and reached to close the door. "Thank you. I've…I've really got to go."

The woman stepped back and Brittney finally managed to get the door closed. She hit the automatic lock, discovered her car was still running, then put the engine into reverse, her only intention to get as far as she could, as fast as she could, away from Deeb's nonexistent house.…

CHAPTER THREE

NATALIE HAD IMMEDIATELY responded to the firefighter's call for help, but was forced to step back as the young woman—who had been all but unconscious a moment before—sped off in reverse. Twenty or so feet down the highway, she spun the rusted vehicle around, then raced off into the rain.

"What do you make of that?" the firefighter asked.

Natalie frowned. "I don't know. Low blood sugar, maybe. Shock." She looked at him. "Did you recognize her?"

"No."

At any rate, there was nothing she could do about the woman now. You could only help those who wanted to be helped.

She found her gaze pulled to Dan Egan's powerful back, the thought ringing even truer.

A plaintive call echoed through the rain. Natalie was pretty sure someone was yelling for help, but given her position at the foot of the mountain, with the waves of the bay crashing against the shore behind her, she couldn't be sure from which direction the cry was coming.

She realized she was still staring at Dan's wide back when she saw another firefighter rush up to his side, pointing out something near the top of the shifting mountain. She squinted against the rain. A man stood on his roof, alternately shouting at the people below and rubbing his chest and left arm. Natalie slowly advanced toward Dan, her umbrella falling back even as she gripped it. Mindless of the rain soaking her hair and face, she watched the stranded man drop to his knees, silent now as he desperately clutched his left arm.

"That's not good," she murmured, coming to stand next to Dan.

"What is it?" he asked.

"He's demonstrating the classic symptoms of cardiac arrest."

Dan's head whipped around, just as a burst of static sounded on the radio he held in his left hand. He lifted it to his ear and fiddled with the knobs before speaking into the mouthpiece. "Come again, HQ."

"Call on the 911 line, Egan. A man says he's trapped on the roof of his house at 432 Truesdale. The mud's rising fast and he's suffering from severe chest pains."

Dan caught and held Natalie's gaze. "Tell him we'll get to him as soon as we can. Out."

Natalie closed her umbrella and headed toward the Jeep for her bag.

"Where do you think you're going?" Dan asked, grasping her arm.

She blinked at him and then at his hand on her arm. "I've got to help him."

Dan's face was drawn into hard lines. "To do that you'd have to get to him first." He pointed to a spot just south of the house the man stood on. "See that? The bridge has been completely washed out. There's no way my team can reach him anytime soon."

Natalie swallowed. This was one of the hardest parts about being a physician—knowing you were trained to help people but not being able to do it. "There's got to be some way. What about air rescue?" She looked up into the glowering sky. "Where's the helicopter?"

"Unfortunately, the pilot's off sick today and it'll take too long to arrange backup."

She stared at Dan, wanting him to do something, anything, to try to remedy the situation.

He seemed to realize he still held her arm. Cursing quietly, he released her and strode away.

Natalie followed on his heels. "What are you going to do?" she asked, fighting to keep up.

"Fly up there myself."

"Then I'm coming with you."

"I'm well trained in handling cardiac arrest cases, Nat."

Nat. He'd called her Nat. No one but her brothers ever referred to her that way. Not even Charles. The familiarity sent warmth skittering over her chilled skin. "Your men have their hands full here. What are you proposing to do? Fly in there alone to take care of the situation?"

He stared at her long and hard, then finally said, "Grab your bag and let's go."

FIFTEEN MINUTES, a slick drive to the airport and a choppy flight later, Dan carefully navigated the medevac helicopter over the mountain. His experience as a helicopter pilot was extensive—he'd flown many emergency missions in the military throughout troubled areas of the world—but it had been awhile since he'd been at the controls.

He glanced at Natalie in the seat next to him, attempting to tune out how white she was. He'd tried to warn her against coming. These types of rescues weren't for the faint of heart. Add in the rain that was coming down in heavy sheets again, and he was surprised the doc was able to keep her lunch down. He spared her slender body a glance. If she'd even eaten lunch.

"Over there!" Natalie shouted at him through the headphones, clearly not used to talking into the pencil-thin black microphone she'd pushed away from her cheek.

Dan spotted the house in question. Mud was rising at a fast rate around the two-story structure, which now looked like a one-story house. The man who had called 911 lay completely still on one side of the flat, Mediterranean-style roof, seemingly unaware of their approach.

"Where are you going?" Natalie asked.

"I have to circle back around and try to land in the clearing just behind the house." Dan tapped the mike in front of his mouth, gesturing for her to move hers so he could hear her. "Let's just pray the ground is solid enough to hold us."

Natalie fiddled with the mike and nodded.

The blast from the helicopter's rotor blades nearly flattened the pines around the small clearing and blew the rain into thick sheets around them. Dan carefully negotiated the landing and powered down the rotor the instant they touched ground while Natalie yanked at her seat harness. After commanding Spike to stay put, Dan opened his door, then reached over and popped the release on hers. He grabbed the rescue equipment and jumped out. She spared him a grateful look before clambering down herself, following in his wake as the chopper's blades spun to a stop.

"Watch your step!" Dan shouted, grabbing hold of her rain slicker with his free hand to keep her from being swept down by a vein of shifting mud. The footing was questionable at best, downright hazardous at worst. He should never have allowed Natalie to come along. But she'd been right that he needed help. Every spare hand he had was busy trying to save those lower on the mountain.

Natalie stopped abruptly, staring at the sight before them.

The mud had risen another several feet and was now almost level with the roof of the house.

"We don't have much time!" he shouted. "We need to get him out of there now!"

"I need to check him first."

"No time for that! If we don't move him now, it will be our bodies they'll be digging out of this mess."

Her pretty face went even paler, if that were possible. Dan helped her navigate the roof, then he set the lightweight stretcher next to their patient. If he had to, he could drag the guy out himself.

"He still has a pulse," Natalie called, fastening an oxygen mask over the man's mouth and nose. "Faint but sure."

"Get his feet."

Natalie grabbed the unconscious man's ankles.

"On the count of three. One, two, three…"

Up and onto the stretcher he went.

Dan made quick work of strapping the victim onto the stretcher, while Natalie fastened a portable defibrillator to his chest.

"Let's go!" he shouted.

Together they carried the man across the roof and onto the shifting ground. A loud gasp made Dan look back in time to see Natalie lose her footing as mud oozed around the boots she'd found in the back of the chopper. A sea of mud was welling around the roof they'd just left.

Releasing his grasp on the stretcher, he helped her pull herself free from the sucking mud, then they both ran for the helicopter, lugging the stretcher between them. They slid it into the back of the copter and the metal clamps clicked home.

"Leave the helmet. Just secure yourself!" Dan shouted, hoisting Natalie into the chopper. He didn't feel good about this. He didn't feel good about it at all.

Quickly he climbed into the cockpit and pressed the ignition, even as Natalie took the seat next to him, fastening the harness.

He watched as mud rushed over the landing skids of the chopper. Jesus…

"Hold on!" With a flip of a switch and a jerk on the cylindrical stick between his legs, they were airborne.

As soon as the helicopter was stable, Dan glanced back to find no sign of the roof, just a relentless river of mud.

THE CHOPPER SAT ready for liftoff on the Courage Bay Hospital's helipad. The patient had been stabilized and was now in the hospital staff's capable hands.

The rush of adrenaline that had kept Natalie going plummeted, almost making her dizzy as she fastened herself back into her seat. She was soaked to the skin, and the seat belt bit into her shoulders, but she felt an odd sense of euphoria at having rushed into the fray with Dan and saved a man's life.

"The attending doc says he's going to pull through." Dan's voice came over the headphones as he powered up the helicopter once more.

Natalie remembered to tug her mike in front of her mouth as she nodded at him. The chopper gave a lurch and they were again airborne.

They were going to take the helicopter back to the airport, where they would retrieve Dan's Jeep. Natalie had been half afraid he would suggest she stay at the hospital and not make the return trip with him, but thankfully, he hadn't said anything. She suspected he was totally focused on getting back to the mudslide and relieving the squad's captain he'd left in charge.

During their flight to the hospital, the storm had let up a bit. Rain was still coming down heavily, but the winds had died down—for the time being, anyway.

Natalie watched as the white X of the hospital's landing pad grew farther and farther away beneath them. She'd worked at the hospital for more than ten years, but she'd never seen it from this angle. Through the pounding rain it looked almost surreal.

Who was she kidding? This entire experience had been surreal. She'd never been up in a helicopter before, yet she had helped Dan rescue an ill man from his roof moments before the mudslide had claimed the entire house.

A curse filled her ears.

She turned to look at Dan. His right hand was fused to the stick between his powerful legs, his left to a longer one between their seats, which looked like an oversize emergency brake. His right hand and the stick it held shuddered ominously.

"What's wrong?" she asked.

Deep grooves bracketed his mouth as he flicked his gaze from the instrument panel, with its hundreds of dials and switches, to the windshield. "The winds are picking up and I see thunderheads rolling in. The storm's switched course and is circling around behind us."

Natalie looked back over her shoulder. Ominous black clouds pillowed bright, jagged shafts of lightning. She could no longer make out the hospital in the dimming light.

"It's unsafe to try to land back at the hospital," Dan said through the mike. "My best bet is to try to go around the storm and approach the airport from the northwest." He spared her a quick glance, his blue eyes lingering for a moment before shifting back to the instrument panel. "Hold on."

Natalie grasped her harness for dear life as he made a sharp right turn. The wind pushed at the helicopter relentlessly, making it sway in the air.

She closed her eyes and took a deep breath. Earlier, she'd been so focused on the rescue that she hadn't really stopped to think how dangerous it was to be flying in these conditions. But when the helicopter hit an air pocket and dropped a few yards, she could have sworn her stomach pitched down, too—somewhere in the vicinity of her icy, boot-clad feet.

Her feet? She suspected her heart had just hit the ground some thousand feet below. Until it came boomeranging back up with a vengeance and lodged in her throat.

In the distance, lightning split the dark sky—in front of them this time, making her jump. This couldn't be safe! Thunder rattled the windshield of the small aircraft as it was buffeted by the storm.

Natalie leaned closer to the side window, staring down at the darkness below. Another crack of lightning showed her they were above Courage Bay. The high, churning, foam-capped waves revealed that the storm had gone from bad to much, much worse.

She briefly closed her eyes and counted backward from ten. After what she'd seen of Dan and his amazing capabilities today, she wanted to trust him, longed to believe that he would see them through this okay. But this brutal weather, the suddenly very small helicopter, the countless B disaster movies she rented to help make the lonely nights go by, all combined to make her the most frightened she'd been since—well, in her entire life.

Another sharp dip jolted them. The *whump-whump* of the helicopter blades above them, a loud clap of thunder behind, the pounding sound of rain against the windshield and the steady hammering of her heart made her feel as if she was going to be sick.

Another crack of lightning. Only this time it wasn't far off in the distance, but directly in front of them. And just before it disappeared into the dark sky, the helicopter ran straight into its path.

Dan reached a hand out to cup the back of her neck, then pushed her head between her legs. "Hold on. We're going down...."

CHAPTER FOUR

THIS WAS NOT the way he intended to go.

Dan struggled with the helicopter controls. The electrical system was on the fritz after the lightning strike. The aircraft's engine cut on and off as if someone were gunning, then releasing the gas pedal of a car, while the rotor above him continued to spin. He eyed the rpm gauge on the console, watching the needle dive downward. Sheets of rain impeded Dan's vision and his heart slammed against his rib cage. But he knew one thing for sure: this was not going to end him.

"Medevac One, this is air traffic control." A woman's staticky voice came over his headphones. "The Emergency Alert System has been activated. Repeat, the EAS has been activated. Please—"

A loud crackling cut off the transmission.

Damn.

The radio had either shorted out or was fried. His guess was the latter.

"Dan?"

He glanced over at Natalie, having forgotten for

a moment that she was in the chopper with him. Although how he could have done so was a mystery to him. Her mocha-colored eyes were bigger and more mesmerizing in her pale face when shadowed with fear. Spike was cushioned against her side, and she had her arm around him. The sight sent warmth coursing through Dan's bloodstream.

He reached behind him for a thermal blanket and tossed it across her slender legs. "Put your head in your lap, Natalie. I'm going to have to put this bird down and it's not going to be pretty."

That was if he could find a clear, safe spot to land her.

As the helicopter rocked like an amusement park ride whose cable was unraveling, he sought a landing site. To the west lay the rough, steel-gray waves of the Pacific. To the east were the mountains of Courage Bay, normally beautiful, but treacherous in the current circumstances.

A loud system alarm filled his ears. Dan heard Natalie's gasp as the altimeter warned of a rapid loss of altitude and their quick approach to the horizon. He gripped the stick tightly in his hands and maneuvered the control pedals. Holding both steady, he aimed for a spot directly in the middle of Courage Bay.

NATALIE TRIED TO KEEP her head down, but she'd never been the type to hide beneath the covers when the bogeyman might be lurking under her bed. Only this boogeyman was Mother Nature, and Natalie had never been so scared in her life.

The helicopter's quick descent made her feel eerily weightless and light-headed. There was water everywhere. Nothing but water…

Oh, God, she thought. They were going to crash into the Bay.…

She cuddled Spike close, hoping her arms would help cushion him when they hit. Life jackets. They needed life jackets.…

That was the last thought she had before the craft hit hard, nearly jarring her teeth from her gums. The helicopter bounced, then hit again. It listed to the side, the grinding of metal nearly deafening her as the rotor blades struck something, then came to a stop. She was aware of a scream and distantly realized it was her own.

"Get out!"

Natalie blinked. At the last minute, she *had* closed her eyes and buried her face in the blanket.

Spike wriggled free from her grasp. Natalie stared into Dan's face as he released his own harness and quickly reached to unfasten hers. She couldn't seem to make her fingers work as she stared out of the craft to find they weren't bouncing in the waves like an oversize beach ball, but instead were resting on solid ground.

How that was possible was a welcome mystery.

Dan reached across her and opened her door, shoving her outside without preamble. Natalie fell to the wet sand, her bones shuddering as she fought to get to her feet under the pressure of the gale-force winds. Spike jumped out after her, and Dan followed.

"Help me secure her."

Secure her...

A wild gust of wind caught the chopper on the beach, sending it listing to the other side. Dan rushed to the door and reached inside to pull out a rope. "Here!" he shouted over the roar of the storm. "Secure this to a tree. A solid one as far inland as possible."

Natalie blinked against the rain stinging her eyes, and stumbled toward a grove of old pines bent nearly horizontal from the force of the storm. Movement out of the corner of her eye made her jump. She scanned the thick forest. There—to the right! She tried to blink the object into focus, but saw nothing but nature battling nature.

She chose the thickest, oldest pine and ran the rope around the trunk. But as she stood staring at the cord in her hands, she couldn't seem to fix on what kind of knot to tie.

Dan appeared beside her and literally took the decision out of her hands, fastening a simple square knot.

Of course, a square knot.

"Come on!"

She felt him grasp her shoulders, but couldn't

seem to get her feet to cooperate with her own commands, much less Dan's. All she could think of was that they were all right. They were okay. They were not dead. They were very much alive.

"Where are we?" she whispered, the storm stealing her voice away.

"S-hamala Island."

Natalie tried to grasp his words. They were on S-hamala Island—a tiny stretch of land in the middle of Courage Bay that she could see from her apartment window on a clear day. She knew precious little about it except that its name referred to the local Chumash Indians. S-hamala was one of the few islands in Southern California that maintained its original Indian name, and it wasn't open to the public because a number of protected brown pelicans called the south side home.

"There's a coast guard station here," Dan said. "They should be able to help us."

She nodded. Or at least she thought she did. Right that minute, the only thing she could be sure of was that she was upright, that she was alive and that Dan Egan had his arm around her.

CORRECTION, coast guard personnel would be able to help them if anyone was still there. And Dan had the unsettling feeling no one was.

It was standard operating procedure that, given enough advance warning, the remote location be abandoned in favor of the mainland station when severe storms occurred. Dan also knew that rescue craft and personnel had been lost before in storms half as bad as this one was turning out to be.

He squinted into the wind, noting the lack of boats secured to the pier. Nor was there any sign of coast guard staff. If anyone was there, they would have heard the chopper.

Natalie's soft, wet body curved against his, making him all too aware of her presence. Spike lumbered ahead of them, his coat soaked and matted, his tongue lolling out of his mouth as he climbed the steps to the station, which was little more than a small cabin built against a cliff, stilts supporting the front, the rock face comprising the back wall.

"Watch your step," he told Natalie as they began ascending the twenty or so slick wooden stairs. Spike lost his footing ahead of them and Dan gave him a gentle boost, pushing him up to the observation deck that jutted out over the beach.

Locked. The door was locked.

"Stand back," he told Natalie.

She blinked at him in a way that only confirmed his suspicions: she was in shock. He helped her move a few feet to the side. Shrugging out of his windbreaker, he wrapped the sturdy nylon around his hand and smacked the windowpane closest to the door handle. It broke easily and he cleared away the shards of glass, reaching in to free the lock. The wind instantly pushed the wooden door open, slamming it against the inside wall.

Dan hustled Natalie into the dark, empty station, then fought to close and lock the door behind them.

Ineffectually swiping her dark hair from her face, she asked, "Where...where is everybody?"

Dan grimaced as he looked around. "They must have been summoned to the mainland when the storm hit."

He tried the light switches by the door. Nothing. Methodically he made his way to the far wall and tried the radio, which was no more than a hulking shadow. No power.

"I have to go out and find the generator," he said to her.

Natalie stood in the same spot he had left her, just inside the door. The wind and rain whipped through the broken window, causing an almost mournful howling. Spike circled the room, his nails clicking on the wooden planks. At last he sat down next to Natalie and gazed up at her.

"We need to get you out of those wet things," Dan said quietly, concern for her well-being overriding the voice inside his head that warned him to stay away from her. He went to stand in front of her, removing her raincoat, then bending down to help her out of her borrowed boots. Her wet stockings felt surprisingly warm and soft under his fingertips, even as her skirt dripped rainwater onto his hands. He was suddenly filled with the desire to skim his fingers up the length of her shapely legs and help her out of the panty hose…. He jerked his hands back and stood again.

"I'm going out to start the generator."

She nodded, her eyes unnaturally large in her pale face.

Damn, but she was beautiful. And despite the shock that had settled over her when they'd crash-landed, more courageous than most women he knew. She hadn't flinched as the helicopter wove through the rough air currents. Despite the mudslide, she'd jumped right in to rescue the heart attack victim, her movements quick and efficient, her mind clearly on the task at hand. And even in shock she had managed to find the best tree to secure the rope that he hoped would keep the helicopter from being blown out to sea.

Natalie blinked at him, making Dan realize he was staring.

"Why are you smiling like that?" she asked in a small voice.

Smiling? Was he smiling? He cleared his throat and averted his gaze. "I was just thinking how good you were out there, and wondering if maybe you got into the wrong line of work."

At the mere mention of Natalie's work, the burn scar on Dan's side let him know it didn't appreciate the extra tension he'd put on it. It throbbed and pulled and made every move painful.

Surprisingly, Natalie gave him a small smile of her own. "No. No, I think I'm in the right profession."

He waited for her to offer more, but she didn't. Probably still in shock.

"Hopefully I'll be back in fifteen," he said, glancing around the place. "Strip out of the rest of your clothes and find a blanket to dry off with. Warm yourself up."

She nodded.

His fingers were on the door handle when she said his name.

Dan looked over his shoulder.

"Do you need any help?" she asked.

He looked at her standing in the middle of the floor, dripping wet and cold. The woman couldn't seem to stop shivering, yet she'd thought to offer him assistance.

He shook his head. "I think I can handle it."

Then he went outside and quickly closed the door, glad for the wind that ripped his breath from his body and the rain that soaked his face. They made him stop thinking about how much he'd like to kiss the lady doc in the room behind him.

NATALIE SHUDDERED as the door slammed shut. Every part of her seemed to shiver, from the wet bangs hanging above her eyes to her toenails.

The dog sitting next to her whined softly. She blinked his dim shape into focus and slowly reached down to pat him. "We need to dry you off, buddy."

What had Dan said his name was, back at the fire station? Spike. Not Spot. The dog's grandfather had been named Spot.

She stopped her ridiculous thoughts and bent to pick up her boots and coat, moving them from the center of the room closer to the door. She'd have to look for something to tack up over the broken pane. The howling of the wind through the narrow opening made her shiver more than her wet clothing did.

Slowly, methodically, she made her way around the small cabin, finding a cot, the communications radio, a table and four chairs, and a row of cabinets built into the far wall. She crouched down and began opening and closing cabinet doors until she found an oil lantern. She shook it, heard the promising slosh of fuel inside, then lifted it to the counter, switching her attention to the drawers and a search for matches. Within moments a warm yellow glow fought the approaching night.

Despite the warmth of Southern California in the winter, the sun still set at 5:00 p.m. Here on the island, the temperature would be even chillier than the mainland, storm or no storm.

And Dan was outside without so much as a flashlight.

Using the lantern to guide her way, Natalie found a small stack of blankets, T-shirts and khaki pants in a storage closet. The clothes were likely extras for coast guard personnel. She glanced over her shoulder at the door and curtainless windows before peeling her wet blouse and skirt from her body, followed by her bra, nylons and panties. She made quick work of drying herself with one of the blankets, then pulled on an oversize T-shirt, as well as a pair of pants, rolling up the waist of the khakis until they stopped sliding down her narrow hips. By the time she'd dried her hair, she was feeling marginally better.

After hanging her own clothes over a chair, she bent to dry Spike. The old dog licked her face in gratitude.

Natalie smiled. That was the best thing about dogs. You never had to wonder how they felt about you.

Her hands slowed their movements on the dog's fur as she questioned her choice of words. She remembered Dan's face when he'd knelt in front of her minutes ago, his fingers strong and warm against her ankles as he'd helped remove her wet shoes. He'd lingered there, and the storm had seemed to grow quiet as a shiver of a whole different variety worked its way over Natalie's skin.

She'd known a moment of longing so strong it had rocked her to the core.

And scared her beyond belief.

Then Dan had pulled away and she'd forced aside the thought of his being interested in her, and her own startling attraction to him.

Until he'd grinned at her....

Natalie closed her eyes and swallowed hard. Dan had looked at her the way Charles once had. His features soft. His eyes warm. His smile genuine....

Spike nudged her chin, reminding her that she was neglecting her duties.

Natalie wrinkled her nose at the wet dog smell and finished drying him with a quick flourish. "Here," she said, finding a rug in front of the sink and pulling it to one side. "Lie down."

The aging dalmatian looked at her and the rug before walking over to it and plopping down right in the middle.

"Good boy." Natalie patted his head.

Long minutes later she'd found another couple of lanterns partially filled with fuel. She put them on the counter but resisted the urge to light them, no matter how dark and scary the night. Instead she busied herself cutting a piece of cardboard from the side of the box that had held the T-shirts. When she'd finished, she took the lantern with her to the door and fastened the cardboard over the broken window with duct tape. The howling immediately ceased. With a deep sigh she stepped to the window beside the door and stared out into the stormy night.

She could hear the crashing of the waves against the shore a short distance away, but couldn't see them until lightning split the night, eerily illuminating the bay. Like roiling black oil topped with menacing whitecaps, waves assaulted the shore with punishing precision. Somewhere out there in the darkness, Dan was looking for the generator.

A gust of wind shook the cabin and pushed through a corner of her window cover. The flame of the lantern she'd set on the floor flickered in the blast, then went out altogether.

Shivering, Natalie wrapped her arms around herself, wishing she hadn't told Spike to lie down across the room. Wet and smelly as he was, she preferred the dog's company to being alone.

She wanted to believe that the storm and the day's events were to blame for her feeling so utterly and completely alone. But she knew better. The sensation had been following her around for the past year. Longer, if she were to be honest with herself.

She'd heard it said that being alone and being lonely were two different things. That you could be lonely even when you were surrounded by people. And you could be alone and not feel lonely.

Lightning zigzagged across the sky and thunder shook the floor under her feet. She winced, in that one moment feeling more alone *and* lonely than she'd ever felt in her life.

Light flickered inside the station. For a moment she thought it might have been the lightning that had briefly illuminated the room. Moments later she made out the steady hum of a generator, and the light from a single bulb hanging in the middle of the ceiling slowly grew stronger and steadier.

Tightly coiled tension eased from her muscles, and across the room Spike lifted his head as if in approval. Natalie wrapped her arms tighter around her, a different kind of tension filling her at the thought of Dan's imminent return.

She should busy herself, she thought absently. Do something so it wouldn't look as if she was waiting for him. But the simple truth of the matter was that she *was* waiting for him. What else would she be doing?

They'd just crash-landed on a remote, deserted island, and while they were safe, there was no telling how long they would be here. No rescue boat could be sent after them in this storm. And the same went for a plane or helicopter.

Which meant she and Dan would be utterly alone in a room no larger than her bedroom.

Moments later he pushed the door open, then immediately closed it against the wind.

And Natalie realized that not only wasn't she alone any longer, she no longer felt lonely....

CHAPTER FIVE

DAN WAS STARING.

Somewhere in the back of his mind, he knew it to be the case. Realized that he was standing in the middle of the coast guard station looking at Dr. Natalie Giroux as if she'd grown two heads while he'd been away. Or, more accurately, as if she was the most welcome thing he'd seen in a long, long time. But he couldn't seem to help himself. She looked so…different.

His gaze took in the cotton coast guard T-shirt. Though it was at least two sizes too big for her, the gentle slope of her breasts and the evidence of the stiff tips pressing against the soft material told him she wasn't wearing anything underneath. Whatever she'd been doing had hiked the shirt up slightly on her right side, revealing a narrow stretch of pale, flawless skin.

Dan's throat grew tight. It had been a long time since he'd been drawn to a woman the way he was drawn to the lady doc. And the idea that he could be attracted to anyone else, given his love for his late wife, troubled him. Made him more than a little angry.

"I found the generator," he said unnecessarily, filling the silence.

Natalie dropped her eyes and gave him a ghost of a smile. She seemed to catch on to what he'd been looking at, and began plucking the shirt away from where it clung to her damp breasts. "I, um, found some clothes over there in the storage closet. You should get out of those wet things and see if there's something that fits you."

As she spoke, her eyes shifted and she took in the way his own rain-soaked clothes were sticking to his body.

Dan realized that he was cold. The storm and its gale-force winds had sent the temperature lower than the locals were used to. Dan was a Texan by birth. He'd come here some twenty-two years ago, during his stint as a smoke jumper, and had stayed when he'd met and married his wife, Eleanor. He had never made it back to Turning Point, Texas, for more than a visit since. Had really never wanted to...until he'd lost Ellie to breast cancer two years ago. He'd considered returning to the town in which he'd grown up, but he had only to think of his daughter, Debra, whose only home had been Courage Bay, to know he could never leave.

Then, of course, there was also the guilt he felt,

as if merely considering the idea somehow betrayed Ellie's memory.

"Here, why don't I help?"

Dan was surprised to find Natalie standing directly in front of him, unbuttoning his jacket. Her hands were lean and capable and feminine—her wrists so small he thought he could wrap his index finger completely around one. And her hair…

He took a discreet breath of the faint fragrance. The rain-dampened strands smelled of something tart and tangy. Lemony.

She'd opened his jacket and now began pushing it over his shoulders and down his arms, her fingers brushing against his denim shirt underneath, coming too close to his skin for comfort and setting off an interesting series of sensations.

Dan shrugged away from her too tempting touch. "I can do it," he said, sounding gruff even to his own ears.

She blinked those warm brown eyes at him, appearing surprised as she withdrew her suddenly trembling hands. Dan was intrigued by the idea that she didn't want to be attracted to him any more than he wanted to be to her.

It seemed Natalie was battling a few demons of her own.

"I'm sure you can," she said softly.

He watched as she walked back to the window

where he'd first spotted her after he'd switched on the generator. She'd been standing there, staring out at the angry sea. She'd looked so small. So helpless. Two words he would never have thought himself using to describe Dr. Natalie Giroux, who he was trying to convince himself was Nurse Ratched with an advanced degree, if only to dampen his attraction to her. But there you had it. Small and helpless was exactly how she'd looked.

And so damn beautiful his stomach had ached.

Dan grumbled under his breath and headed for the opposite corner of the room. He quickly found a T-shirt and pair of pants to fit him, then stripped off his jeans. His gaze caught on a scrap of purple satin hanging over the back of a nearby chair, and the air froze in his lungs. It seemed a bra wasn't the only thing the lady doc was minus. Leaving his own soaked boxers in place, he pulled on the pants and fastened them, then began unbuttoning his shirt.

Despite the coolness of the wet fabric, it seemed to burn against the wound on his side. The day's activities had put added stress on the tight, puckered skin until he had to grit his teeth against the pain even the simplest of movements caused. But rather than going easy, he yanked up his shirt and began pulling it off with short, impatient jerks.

When he felt cool fingertips against his back, he swiveled around so quickly he nearly lost his balance.

Natalie blinked up at him warily. "Why don't you move into the light so I can take a look?"

Dan stared at her as he groped for the T-shirt he'd left lying on the counter behind him, and pulled it on. "Why don't you accept that I don't need a follow-up appointment?"

Especially not in the dark of night, while they were stranded together on a deserted island.

Especially not when her most innocent of touches set his skin on fire in a way that wasn't connected to his burn scar, and made him long for things he didn't want to think about.

She sighed heavily. "You know, I'd have thought that after all we've been through this afternoon, something like letting me examine the progress of your healing would be a minor consideration."

Dan smoothed back his hair. "Yeah, well, you thought wrong." He stalked over to the communications radio and started flipping switches. The machine was ancient. Thirty years old at best. It was his guess that the crew made the majority of their transmissions via their boat radios rather than through this old thing. The monitoring of the bay and the stretch of Pacific just beyond was the responsibility of the mainland station.

"I'm going to see if I can get word to ScanSoCal on our location and situation. Failing that, hopefully we can reach CAM SPAC, the nerve center of the Pacific Coast Guard. Do you want me to pass a message on to anyone for you?"

Natalie's gaze was fixed on his hand—his left hand. Dan glanced down to find the overhead light glinting off the gold of his wedding band. A ring he hadn't taken off in over twenty-two years. Not since the day he'd vowed to love, honor and cherish Eleanor until death did them part.

When Natalie looked up at him, he saw surprise, confusion and grief in her eyes.

Dan cursed himself. He didn't want to read anything in those eyes.

"No," she said softly.

Fine.

He returned his attention to the radio, flicking switches and tweaking knobs as he searched for Blue 8 at 470.5375 MHz. Loud white static sounded over the speaker. He located the volume control and turned it down. The radio was an old VHF band and its range in this type of a storm would be limited at best.

"ScanSoCal, this is S-hamala Island Coast Guard Station. Repeat, ScanSoCal, this is S-hamala Island Station, do you read?"

Nothing but static answered him, broken only when he pressed the button to transmit.

He tried a couple of other frequencies, the one the Courage Bay fire department monitored among them, but no luck. Since the chopper's radio had been fried by the direct lightning strike, they were essentially flying blind.

His only other option was to try to reach an ACS—Auxiliary Communications Service—volunteer, essentially a guy somewhere out there, probably at home on a ham radio, listening in for those who might need help, and prepared to pass the information on to the proper authorities. Dan knew from firsthand experience that ACSs would be monitoring their radios more diligently now that the Emergency Alert System had been activated. Maybe he'd have better luck getting one of them to respond.

As he went about trying to gain contact with someone, he watched Natalie finally move from the spot where she'd been standing. Her actions were fluid and precise as she searched through the cabinets, coming up with a can of soup, a single-burner propane stove and a pan. Another sweep and she took out a tightly wrapped package of crackers.

Dan hadn't realized he was hungry until that moment.

Of course, he'd feel a whole hell of a lot better if he could convince himself that his pangs were solely for the food Natalie was preparing and not for the pretty lady doc herself.

The sooner he could raise someone—anyone—on this ancient radio, the better.

MULE.

Natalie poured the contents of a can of minestrone into a pan, then added water from one of the bottles in the well-stocked storage closet and stirred. Dan Egan was every bit the stubborn male she'd suspected him to be. His reaction when she'd tried to examine his burn scar had confirmed her suspicion.

She rattled the pan louder than necessary as she put it over the flame of the burner. When she looked to see if Dan had noticed, his attention was on the radio.

"My brothers."

She spoke the words the moment she thought them.

"Did you say something?" Dan asked, the static fading as he turned the volume control down.

Her throat tight, Natalie forced herself to swallow. When he'd first asked if she wanted him to get word out to anyone on her whereabouts, she'd thought of Charles. Partly it had been a knee-jerk reaction. Charles had been involved in her life for more than ten years, although it had only been a short time before his death that they'd decided to marry.

But another reason for her reaction had to do with seeing that Dan still wore his wedding ring, even though his wife had died two years ago.

When she realized her gaze was fused to the ring in question, she looked up into Dan's face. He appeared more than a little put out and also curious as to what she'd said.

"My brothers, Alec and Guy. They're both on staff at Courage Bay Hospital. If you could get word out to them that I'm okay, I'd be thankful."

He squinted at her. "You're all doctors?"

She nodded.

His smile warmed her straight down to her toes. "Yes, they'd probably like to know you're okay."

Natalie smiled back.

The only constants in her otherwise bumpy life had been her brothers. She was the middle child. Guy was six years older, Alec two years younger. But the years separating them had ceased to be a factor when their parents were involved in a car crash when she was nine.

She absently rubbed her neck, not really seeing the soup she was stirring with her other hand. The car accident had happened on a slippery road on a stormy night much like tonight. If it had taken place today, both her parents might still be alive. But air bags hadn't been required in automobiles back then. And even if they had been, who was to say her parents would have gotten out of the car after they hit the large oak tree head-on and before the gas tank exploded?

Her father had died instantly.

Her mother had survived what essentially amounted to hell on earth for four long days, ninety percent of her body covered in fourth-degree burns. Heart-wrenching moans were the only sounds she'd made when she regained consciousness, right before she died.

And then there were three....

It was only years later that Natalie realized how odd it was none of them discussed the fact that they had been in the back seat of the car that fateful night. Their seat belts had prevented major injury, and Guy had had the presence of mind to get the three of them out of the car before it exploded.

She and Guy and Alec had been inseparable after that, even after they'd gone on to live relatively normal lives with their father's brother's family. That each of them had gone into medicine wasn't surprising, she supposed, especially considering that their father had been a doctor himself. What was amazing was that all three of them had managed to grow up to be well-adjusted adults.

Of course, it all depended on your definition of well adjusted, she thought. Her own life had been quite solitary after med school, and both Guy and Alec had experienced failed marriages. At least Alec had now found love with his fiancée, Janice.

Natalie found she was staring at Dan, although he'd

long since returned his attention to the radio. Outside the storm raged. They were separated from everything familiar, yet they were safe and dry and warm.

"S-hamala Island Station, this is Godfrey Kohl in Santa Cruz. I read you loud and clear."

Natalie's every muscle relaxed at the realization they'd made contact. Dan told Kohl who they were, and briefly sketched what had happened, then asked him to pass on a message to the coast guard, the Courage Bay fire department and the hospital.

"Will do," Kohl said after repeating the information and the contact persons. "Is there anything else I can do for you, Chief Egan?"

"It's Dan, please."

There was a pause, then Kohl said, "Okay, then. You can just call me God."

DAN SWITCHED OFF the radio, then ran his hand over his face. Godfrey had informed him that the National Weather Service had put out a severe thunderstorm warning that was expected to last until well into tomorrow.

He sat back and glanced over at Natalie. She had opened a can of corned beef and was spooning out half onto a paper plate for a very grateful Spike.

Dan had been unprepared for his reaction when she'd told him to get a message to her brothers. She had no husband? No boyfriend? No love interest who might be concerned about her whereabouts and condition? He could hardly believe it.

And he found his interest in her personal life intolerable.

He pushed himself up from the chair, checked around the station, then grabbed his wet jeans, heading toward the bathroom he'd spotted off to one side of the room.

"What are you doing?" Natalie asked.

Dan stepped inside the small room, no larger than a closet, and changed back into his jeans while propping the door open. He came back out and put his jacket on over his dry T-shirt. "There's not much fuel left in the generator. I'm going to see if I can find some more." He pulled up the zipper on the jacket. "Failing that, I'm going to have to shut the generator off until tomorrow morning, when maybe the storm will have died down enough for us to contact mainland control."

If part of his decision to get out of the station was the fact he didn't like the direction of his thoughts whenever he was around the lady doc, that was his secret and his alone.

"But I made soup."

Dan glanced at her, glanced at the pan of soup, then handed her one of the lanterns from the counter. "Here, you'll want to light one of these if I can't find more fuel. Go ahead and eat without me."

She looked so genuinely puzzled he felt compelled to curse himself.

In his career, Dan had held positions that demanded fast thinking, quick action, strength and courage, but as soon as his job was done, he'd gone back to the base or the station. The task of what came after fell into someone else's hands.

So facing Natalie now that the action was over was more than a little difficult for him. He had no idea what to say to her.

So he said nothing.

He turned and headed for the door, this time armed with a flashlight.

"Dan?"

His hand hesitated on the doorknob.

"Be careful."

CHAPTER SIX

TWO HOURS LATER Natalie was ready to jump out of her skin.

Despite Dan's telling her to go ahead and eat alone, she hadn't touched the pan of soup still sitting on the portable burner. And twenty minutes after he'd left, the lights had gone off, indicating he hadn't found that extra fuel he'd been looking for. She'd been plunged into darkness, the weak yellow glow from the lantern a far cry from the brightness of the overhead lights.

She paced the floor, trying to ignore the wind that sometimes shook the station around her, and the nonstop lightning strikes that turned the blackness of the night into eerie blue daylight. All of this was so far removed from her normal reality that it felt like some sort of nightmare. After eating his corned beef, Spike had retired to his rug, silent except for the occasional sigh or soft snore. All Natalie had to do was worry about where Dan was and when he might be coming back.

She stepped to the window. She'd grown up

around the sea; her ancestors had settled in the Courage Bay area some hundred and fifty years go. But Natalie had never much liked the Pacific. Water, so much of it, scared her. There was something about the overwhelming size of the ocean that humbled her. Sometimes made her feel that she didn't have a clue about who she was and what she was meant to do.

How could you understand yourself when you couldn't truly understand the larger world around you?

Then she would turn away from the vast ocean to the more familiar waters of Courage Bay and feel all right again.

Courage Bay was smaller. Manageable.

But tonight even the waves in the bay rose up like some sort of prehistoric, mythological sea monster intent on destroying all in its path.

She shuddered along with the wooden planks of the station as another thunderbolt hit somewhere off in the distance, illuminating sea and sky.

"Oh, for Pete's sake, stop it," she whispered to herself.

She thought she detected movement outside the cabin. She leaned closer to the window, trying to see through the lashing rain. Her breath fogged the windowpane, so she used the hem of the T-shirt to clear a hole. All she could make out were the roiling waves and the pines swaying off to her right.

She dropped her arm to her side, knowing a moment of panic. What if something had happened to Dan? What if he was trapped out in that storm with no way to help himself?

Her watch wasn't waterproof and the crystal had fogged from the inside. But she could still make out the time—two minutes later than the last time she'd checked.

A half hour longer. That was all she'd give him. If he wasn't back by then, she'd go outside and look for him.

Turning around, she considered the sleeping dog and the dimly lit station. She couldn't possibly eat. And sleep was definitely out of the question. Since the radio wouldn't work without the generator…

The radio.

She'd seen a weather band radio in one of the cabinets. But which one?

She crossed the room and methodically searched them, finding the radio in the last one. Not even bothering to take it to the table, she sat down on the floor and pressed her thumb against the power switch. She took a deep breath, sent up a silent prayer that the radio had working batteries, then flicked it on.

Static filled the room.

Natalie immediately crossed her legs, looked over the myriad knobs and switches lining the front, then found the tuner. She slowly began turning it, hoping something would pop up.

The sound of quickly spoken Spanish battled with the static.

She turned the radio over, found an antenna tucked away and pulled it out. Deciding that reception might be better if she wasn't on the floor, she stood up and stepped to the front of the cabin before once again turning the dial, slowly, slowly.

"...the weather front battering the western...of Courage Bay..."

Relief flushed through Natalie. All at once she was no longer alone. No longer afraid. She had the human voice on the radio to keep her company.

Now if she could only do something about the worry gnawing at her about Dan's whereabouts...

THERE WAS SOMETHING ABOUT the raw power of nature that appealed to Dan's darker side. Whether it was a forest fire or house fire, or the current storm pounding him from all sides, he liked the fact he didn't have much time to think. Survival depended merely on doing.

After fruitlessly searching for fuel under the coast guard station, he'd decided to have a look around, see if there was a storage shed nearby where extra fuel might be kept. He'd found one some thirty yards northwest of the station, but it was filled with life jackets and doughnut preservers, ropes and buoys. No fuel cans, empty or full anywhere, which struck him as odd. Surely the coast guard personnel would have extra fuel somewhere to keep the station generator going.

When he'd exited the shed, the storm had been raging even harder. He'd been forced to wait inside for a few minutes until it eased. Only it had taken half an hour before he could walk and breathe at the same time. He'd started back for the station only to stop dead in his tracks at the sight of Natalie waiting at the window, the soft glow of a lantern lighting her from behind, reminding him of why he'd headed out in the first place. Sure, he'd needed to look for fuel, but he could have eaten first. Sat with her for a bit.

But he'd found the violent storm easier to take than the lady doc's quiet beauty, and had instead headed out to the beach to check on the chopper.

He'd never been with a woman other than Eleanor. Yes, he'd dated before he'd met her. But he and Ellie had been each other's first time. He'd never...touched another woman as he'd touched her. As he found himself increasingly wanting to touch Natalie Giroux.

It wasn't so much what she said or did; if anything, both would have put him off. But the moment he'd regained consciousness three months ago and caught sight of her mocha-colored eyes above her surgical mask, he'd felt a sensation so utterly foreign to him, so overwhelming that for a minute it had been difficult to breathe.

His balance faltered as he knelt inside the rocking helicopter, collecting things they might need. The wind had picked up again. He packed the items he'd gathered into a duffel bag, then pushed open the door on the pilot's side. The chopper listed as he hauled himself out, the storm swirling around him. He checked the anchor rope again, then set off for the station. With any luck, Natalie would be asleep by now.

Instead, he opened the door to find her sitting at the table, a weather band radio spitting out news of the storm, the transmission cutting in and out.

She instantly stood and turned to face him, making his stomach tighten.

And making him wish he could turn around and head back outside again.

He tore his gaze from her face and moved toward the counter, putting the bag down. "I picked up some things from the chopper while I was out there." He winced, not sure why he'd offered the information or how he felt about doing so. He didn't owe her an explanation.

She wasn't his wife.

"No fuel?"

He glanced at her.

"For the generator. You didn't find any fuel?"

He shrugged out of the jacket, surprised to find the T-shirt underneath still dry for the most part. "No."

Out of the corner of his eye, he saw her wrap her

arms around herself. She seemed to do that a lot around him. "The storm looks like it's getting worse."

He didn't respond. Instead, he moved to the corner where the pants he'd changed out of earlier still hung. He didn't even glance her way as he changed out of his dripping jeans and put on the dry khakis.

"I found a radio in one of the cabinets. They say they expect the storm to stall over the area for several days."

Dan's fingers froze on the zipper of his pants.

Days...

He might be stuck in this small cabin with Natalie for days.

The mere idea made him want to go back outside and take his chances in the storm.

After pulling the zipper, he turned to find she had her back to him, her fingers holding her sides.

"I can only get two radio stations. One's Spanish. But they're pretty much saying the same thing."

He moved up behind her. Her dark hair had dried, but instead of the straight style she'd worn earlier, it was now a riot of soft curls. Ellie's hair had been blond and long. Natalie wore her hair shorter, the ends barely brushing the neckline of her T-shirt.

Hesitantly she turned, starting when she realized he was so close. Her pupils grew large as her gaze lingered on his mouth, then slowly rose back up to his eyes.

Dan swallowed hard.

"Do you mind?" he asked, indicating the radio.

She shook her head.

He plucked it up and switched the band frequency button, quickly turning the tuner, then repeated the action with the other two bands. She was right. Just the two stations.

He put the radio back down and headed for the counter. "Any of that soup left?"

To his dismay, she followed him. "Actually, I was waiting for you to come back before I had any." He looked at her but she avoided his gaze. "I don't like to eat alone," she said quietly.

Dan squinted at her. That was an odd thing to say, wasn't it?

He took the lid off the pan and lit the burner. "Who do you usually eat with?" he asked.

"What?"

He stared at her. "I asked who you usually eat with. Earlier you said your brothers would want to know you were safe, so I assumed…"

She turned away and opened the flap of the bag he'd brought in. "You assumed that I'm single. You assumed right."

Which didn't answer his earlier question about whom she would have eaten with, but hey, he wasn't going to push the issue.

He glanced over at Spike, asleep on a nearby rug.

The old dog hadn't bounded up when Dan had come back into the station. That was becoming more and more the case the older the dalmatian got. The day had probably taken a lot out of him.

"I fed him corned beef earlier," Natalie said.

Dan returned his attention to the soup. "I saw. Thanks."

She gestured toward his hands. "I notice you still wear your wedding band."

Uncomfortable questions. That's why he felt uneasy around the lady doc. If she wasn't trying to get a look at his burn, threatening to touch him with her soft hands, she was asking him things he'd prefer not to talk about. Preferred not to think of.

Still, he found himself considering the bit of gold on his ring finger that had become as much a part of him as a limb.

Of course she would know about his wife. Natalie and Debra were friends of a kind. His daughter had told him Natalie took some aerobics courses at her health club.

He found his gaze straying from his ring to Natalie's slender frame. She was too thin. He doubted she weighed more than a buck-twenty, and given her height, that meant she didn't have very many curves. Her breasts were on the small side, her hips nearly nonexistent. Still, there was an energy about her. And while normally he might find her lack of curves unattractive, right now his body knew a longing to fold her into his arms and explore every hollow and angle.

He found her staring at him and realized that he hadn't responded to her comment about his wedding ring.

And he wasn't going to.

"Are there any bowls?" he asked. "Something we can put this in?"

She blinked, apparently surprised by the change in subject. He supposed she expected to get an answer when she asked a question. But she was going to have to get used to a different response from him.

"Um, I suppose we can use coffee mugs." She collected a couple of larger ones from a cabinet and put them next to the burner.

He poured soup into each mug, then carried them both to the table, placing hers on the opposite side, as far away from his as he could.

She quietly sat down and they ate in silence for long moments, the crackers still on the counter, forgotten. A tension Dan didn't know what to do about infused his every muscle.

Then Natalie cleared her throat and said, "This is the first time in a long time that I'm going to spend the night with a man...."

CHAPTER SEVEN

AWKWARD SITUATIONS WERE fertile ground for stupid comments.

Natalie didn't realize exactly what she'd said until Dan nearly choked on his soup and stared at her as if she'd just suggested they strip down to nothing and go for a skinny-dip in the storm.

The first time in a long time she'd spent the night with a man, indeed.

She'd been trying to make conversation.

Instead, she'd succeeded in making herself look like a needy fool.

"That didn't quite come out the way I intended." She cleared her throat again, then picked up her mug, the soup cool enough to drink now. Or at least she hoped so. "I certainly didn't mean…you know, that we were going to spend the night together…"

She flinched. She was rambling now, and she never rambled. She was a thirty-seven year old doctor, a competent burn specialist, not a nineteen-year-old out on her first real date.

Then why, Natalie wondered, was that exactly how she felt?

Of course, it didn't help that Dan's cool indifference was making her nervous.

Or that he was a very big, very attractive man, and the instant he stepped into a room, she felt his presence like a caress to her skin.

She concentrated on her soup, which was disappearing fast.

"Obviously you already know my story," Dan said, surprising her. "Tell me why you don't have anybody at home waiting for you?"

Okay...

She'd asked for conversation and he was giving it to her.

Why did she have the feeling she was going to be wishing for silence again very soon?

What should she tell him first? That today would have marked her one-year wedding anniversary? That Charles had died a week before the planned event? Or should she go back even further than that, to when she'd faced a choice between marriage and career and had chosen the latter?

"My fiancé died just over a year ago," she said quietly.

She felt Dan's gaze on her face but didn't acknowledge it. Instead, she pretended an interest in her mug of soup. "Heart attack," she added.

Long pregnant moments followed until she could no longer stand the silence.

She looked up to find Dan had stopped eating, and his full attention was on her.

"I'm sorry," he said.

And she felt that he genuinely was.

Then again, if anyone could understand the heartache of losing someone, Dan Egan could.

"Thanks," she said quietly, looking at her own bare ring finger.

For a long time after losing Charles, she'd kept wearing her solitaire engagement ring. The wedding rings she and Charles were to exchange sat tucked deep in the back of her underwear drawer. She was always startled when she happened across the boxes, then would sit on her bed with them open in her hands, crying over what could have been—what should have been—if only Charles had heeded the warnings his body was trying to communicate.

His stubbornness reminded her of another man. The one across from her. The virile fire chief who refused to allow her to examine his burn to determine how deep the wound had gone. And while he wouldn't die from his injury, severe complications could develop as a result of his pigheadedness. If he was experiencing pain, he might be moving in a way that wouldn't impact the wound too much, and as a result, overcompensating with other areas of his body, putting strain on bones and muscles and joints that weren't equipped to deal with the extra load. Especially considering the physical nature of his job.

"You know, sometimes it's difficult to remember her face."

Natalie stared at Dan, unable to believe he'd said what he had.

But he wasn't looking at her. He was staring at his large fingers, white against his mug of soup.

He shrugged his hulking shoulders. "I tell myself it's only natural, you know. I mean, it's been two years. But..."

Before Natalie knew what she was doing, she reached out and placed her hand over his free one, which rested on the table.

His skin was hot to the touch, and she wondered at how small her fingers looked in comparison with his.

He abruptly got up and walked to the small sink.

Natalie sat still for a long moment, then stood up and followed him.

"I think it is," she said quietly, reaching around to put her mug next to his in the sink, not touching him but doing the next closest thing. "Natural, that is."

"I don't know why I told you that," he said gruffly, every bit the strong alpha male bent on pretending he didn't have a soft side. Driven to prove that the fact he sometimes couldn't remember his late wife's face didn't upset him.

"How long were you married?" she asked his back, though she already roughly knew, given his daughter Debra's age.

Natalie saw him stiffen, then start to wash out the cup and the pan. "I think I've had enough of show and tell for one night." He quirked a brow. "Haven't you?"

She didn't blink as she met his even stare. "What else is there to do?"

"Sleep," he said simply, then strode across the room to the storage closet.

DAN SET UP A SECOND COT he found inside the closet, then moved it to the opposite side of the room from the one he'd assembled for Natalie.

Not that it mattered. The room was so narrow that anywhere he put his cot would be too damn close to the lady doc's.

His movements were jerky and impatient, mirroring the emotions blowing around inside him, not unlike the storm outside. Why had he said what he had? At first he'd believed he'd just thought the words. But given the way Natalie's face had paled, he'd realized he'd said them aloud.

And it made him feel as if he'd betrayed his late wife and his daughter in the worst way.

"Here."

He turned to find Natalie standing behind him, ever efficient with a blanket and life preserver. She held up the preserver. "I thought we might use them for pillows."

Good thinking.

He thanked her, then went about making up his cot, although very little needed to be done except for him to lie down on top of it and cover himself.

When Natalie's cot creaked softly, he realized he'd been waiting for her to lie down first.

Dan crossed to the table and picked up the lantern to extinguish the flame.

"Can we leave it burning?" she asked. "Just on low? I'm afraid I'm going to wake up in the middle of the night and not know where I am."

He nodded and placed the lantern near the head of her cot. He wasn't overly concerned about running out of lamp oil. At daybreak they should have enough light to see by, however dim.

"Thanks."

"Don't mention it."

Dan sat down on his cot, his bare feet feeling odd against the rough wooden planks of the floor. He stayed like that for long moments, listening to the wind outside, to Spike's even breathing, and trying not to look at the soft outline of the woman lying across the room.

Finally he stretched out and stared up at the ceiling, the blanket still folded at the foot of the cot.

The first time he'd drawn a blank when he tried

to recall Eleanor's beloved features had been ten months after her funeral. He remembered the panic he'd felt, the complete sense of shame and guilt. She'd been his wife for so long, given so much of herself to their family, surely she deserved to be remembered by him.

The experience had sent him on a hunt for pictures of her. Aside from a faded school photo of Debra that he'd kept tucked in his wallet since she was in the third grade, he wasn't a big picture carrier. But out of desperation he'd slid three photos of Ellie in behind Debra's. And every now and again, as the edges of the memories of his wife began to blur, he pulled the pictures out and stared at them until he was sure the images were burned into his retinas.

And still he forgot....

"Twenty years."

His words seemed to echo throughout the small cabin despite the roar of the storm outside.

Dan heard Natalie shift on her cot, and he could feel her gaze on him in the darkness.

"That's how long Ellie and I were married before...before she passed," he clarified.

After a long silence, Natalie said quietly, "That's a long time."

It was an entire lifetime. His lifetime, brought to an end by three devastating words on that fateful day four years ago, when Ellie had returned from what he'd thought was a regular physical examination, but had instead been the conclusion of a series of medical appointments she'd been going to without anyone knowing. *I have cancer.*

While Dan might not have total recall of his wife's facial features, the way he'd felt in that moment would be with him always.

"Today would have been my one-year anniversary." Natalie's voice broke the silence that had filled the small cabin. "I know it sounds insignificant in light of what you've gone through...."

Dan turned his head and tried to make her out in the darkness. She lay on her side, facing him, but just like the memories of his wife, her features were in shadow, indistinguishable.

"I'd waited so long to get married, and...well..."

Her words trailed off.

"Why?"

Another silence, then he heard her shift, rearranging her blanket. "Why did I wait so long to get married?" He had the feeling she was sounding out the question rather than asking for verification, so he didn't say anything. "I don't know. I mean, the reasons seemed valid enough back then. For a long, long time I wanted to be a doctor. Not just a regular doctor but a burn specialist. And that takes a lot of dedication and training. I also did a residency stint at the MetroHealth Medical Center in Cleveland, Ohio.

And, well, in the end, my schooling and specialized residency didn't leave a lot of time for a relationship."

Dan pondered the differences between the doc and his wife. Aside from a brief stint as a waitress when he'd first met Ellie, she had never worked outside the home once they'd married. Her job had been to look after the house, him and their daughter, not necessarily in that order. When he'd come home, there'd always been food cooking or a plate kept warm for him. His clothes had always been neatly tucked into his drawers, his shirts and pants pressed, his newspaper waiting on the kitchen table, where Ellie would put a cup of coffee or a beer, depending on what time of day it was. She'd attended all of Debra's school activities when he couldn't, had gone to the parent-teacher meetings, had enrolled, then driven Debra to all her dance classes. Ellie had kept the peace not only between him and her family, but with his family in Turning Point when his "I'll call next week" turned into next month, then the next.

Eleanor had once told him she didn't know how working mothers did it. Her day was so full that she couldn't have squeezed out time for a part-time job, much less a full-time one.

Obviously Natalie had come to the same conclusion Eleanor had. Only Dr. Natalie Giroux had chosen a different route.

"Do you ever regret it?" he asked quietly. "Not marrying sooner?"

Long seconds ticked by. "All the time," she whispered. "If Charles and I had planned the wedding for even a few months sooner, maybe he'd still be here."

Dan made the necessary maneuvers on the narrow cot so that he could lie facing her. He winced when his scar pulled tight, sending shooting pains down his side. "I don't mean just now…recently. I'm talking about when you were younger."

Even though he couldn't see her eyes, he felt a connection with her that made him feel warm.

"Do you ever regret marrying your wife?"

That took him aback. What would make her ask something like that? "No. Never."

She didn't say anything for a long moment, then murmured, "That's my answer to your question."

Dan mulled that one over, still shell-shocked. "Hell of a way to make your point."

He swore she was smiling. "I'm sorry. It's just that I get questions like yours all the time. It almost feels like I'm some sort of human experiment everyone wants to study. I guess in the end, even now in the twenty-first century, the feminine mystique is still alive and well." She blew out a long breath. "You have no idea how many times I've seen pity in the eyes of others when they realize that I've never married and don't have children." She shifted again, making him aware of her in ways he preferred not to explore just then.

And making him wish he hadn't moved his cot so far away.

"So many people think I've sacrificed my life for medicine. I prefer to think that I've enriched my life with medicine."

Dan chewed on that for a while, thinking of the ways their lives differed. Nearly everyone he knew his and Natalie's age were married or divorced. And most of them had children. Choosing a career didn't necessarily mean the exclusion of everything else.

But perhaps for a woman, the decision was a little more complicated.

"What do you do in the middle of the night when your feet are cold?" he asked quietly.

Her quick intake of breath told him his question had caught her off guard.

"Now that's a question I haven't heard before," she said, plainly amused. "That's an easy one. I put on a pair of socks."

Dan grinned, imagining the lady doc wearing a flannel nightgown and donning thick wool socks.

Strangely, the image was a sexy one.

Doubly strange, he was coming to think anything connected to Natalie from now on would be sexy to him. Which was the main reason he didn't want her poking at him. Not at his scar. Not at his life.

In the days before Ellie died, she'd said something to him that still haunted him.

"I want you to marry again, Dan."

Ellie had been undergoing intensive chemotherapy sessions combined with spot radiation, but the cancer was winning. They'd all known it. And they'd all accepted it in their own way, even if they didn't admit it to each other. Eleanor was going to die and there was nothing Dan, Debra or Ellie herself could do about it.

Still, he'd been so wholly unprepared for what she'd said that, even now, something akin to razor wire twisted deep in his stomach.

"Never," he'd told her.

His wife had simply smiled at him in that gentle way of hers and asked him to sit next to her on the bed. "Dan, you were made to be a husband and father."

He'd looked deep into her pain-filled, beautiful blue eyes and told her he was made to love her....

"You have only the one child—Debra—right?" Natalie's voice reminded him that he wasn't at home alone in his bed, having just woken up from the nightmare that had haunted him for what seemed like forever.

"Yes." He rolled over, away from her, ignoring the pain down his back and side, and the pain of other wounds that ran so deep no doctor would be able to heal them. Not even Natalie. "Good night," he said purposefully.

Silence, then, "Good night."

CHAPTER EIGHT

NATALIE HUDDLED UNDER the blanket, the storm outside sneaking inside her dream and taking the shape of a harsh white wind that carried Charles slowly, torturously away from her even as she tried to hold on to him. Then he was gone and she was surrounded by thick white fog. No, not fog. Mist. Then the wind whipped at the white wisps and she searched for Charles, only he wasn't there. In his place stood Dan Egan, his handsome face somber, his arms open wide.

Natalie jerked awake, out of breath, a thin sheen of sweat coating her skin. The wool blanket was too warm, the air thick and humid, the sound of the storm still raging outside. She peeled the cover away from her chest and folded it across her hips, staring at a ceiling that wasn't familiar to her. All at once she remembered where she was and everything that had happened yesterday.

Dan...

Pushing up onto her elbows, she blinked into the

gray dimness surrounding her. Daylight. Dan's cot across the room was empty.

She looked down at the T-shirt she was wearing and pulled the blanket back up until she could straighten the shirt where it bunched under her breasts, leaving her stomach bare.

No matter how hard she tried, the image in the dream wouldn't leave her.

As a joke she'd consulted a dream interpreter once, down on the Santa Monica Pier, with several friends from the UCLA Medical Center. She idly wondered what the eccentric old woman would make of the dream she'd just had. Not that it took a certified dream interpreter to figure it out. Obviously her attraction for Dan Egan and the fresh reminder of her loss of Charles with what would have been their one-year anniversary was wreaking havoc on her subconscious.

Dan Egan would never hold his arms out to her, at least not to embrace her. To push her away, maybe, but not to hold her.

She didn't want him to embrace her. He was stubborn and pigheaded and probably deserved the pain she sometimes saw on his face when he moved too quickly. It was obvious his burn wound hadn't healed properly and the scar tissue was causing him a great deal of pain. But until he would let her have a look, there wasn't anything she could do about it.

She pushed her tangled hair back from her face.

Okay, so maybe she would admit that despite his piggish manner, she wouldn't mind being held by the big bear of a man.

Wouldn't mind? At the mere thought, her heart tripped in her chest and her palms grew damp.

A creak sounded above her. She looked up at the ceiling as the bathroom door opened and Dan came out, wearing only the borrowed khaki pants, finger-combing his dark, damp hair. He was built like a bodybuilder, with long, well-defined muscles, and arms that looked as if they could lift a Mack truck. Normally she didn't find overly developed men appealing. After all, she was surrounded by them whenever she went to work out at Debra's gym. But Dan…she couldn't seem to drag her gaze away from his finely honed body. Even if he was obviously making a point of not turning his back to her.

Then it dawned on her that in order to go in and out of the bathroom, he'd had to pass her. Natalie's face burned at the thought of him looking at her while she was sleeping.

"Morning," he said gruffly, taking the "good" out of the greeting.

"Back at you," she mumbled in return.

She squinted through the dim light to catch a glimpse of his scar. But before she knew it, he was at his cot, half turned from her and pulling his T-shirt over his head.

Okay. If that's the way he wanted things, that was just fine with her.

She squinted at her watch but couldn't make out the time.

"It's just after seven."

"Thanks."

She watched as he folded his blanket and placed it on top of the life preserver that had been his pillow. "You wouldn't have happened to come across any coffee yesterday?" he asked.

Natalie checked the integrity of her pants under cover of the blanket, then swung her legs over the side of the cot. "Third drawer to the left. Sugar and creamer's in there, too."

"I like mine black."

"I like mine with sugar and cream. One of each, please."

He stared at her as he moved the cot out of the way.

She ignored him.

Another creak sounded above her. Dan looked up at the same time she did.

The creak morphed into a loud crack, then a crash, as something hit the roof above her.

Before she could blink, Dan had her up in his arms and was standing on the other side of the room, while they both watched the ceiling cave in, covering her cot with debris.

Natalie's heart hammered in her chest.

Not just at the incredible sight she was witnessing, but at the realization she was being held tightly in the very arms she'd been so obsessed with moments ago.

She swallowed hard. She hadn't imagined he'd be so…hard. So warm. So damn big.

As she blinked up into his eyes, she found him looking as startled as she felt and, she suspected, for the very same reasons. His rapidly beating heart also betrayed his reaction to their close proximity. As did the widening of his pupils in his light blue eyes.

Despite the wind howling in through the collapsed roof, the rain soaking the cot and the floor, and the tree limb poking through the hole, Dan's gaze dropped to her mouth. Natalie slowly licked her lips, her stomach filling with tension and desire for a man she had no business desiring.

But tell that to her traitorous body.

His gaze moved back to her eyes and he looked as if he had just snapped out of a trance. "Are you okay?"

She nodded, incapable of words at the moment.

He moved to put her down on her feet and she wanted to protest.

But she said nothing, and within moments they stood facing each other. Natalie felt as if the temperature had dropped a good ten degrees.

Dan ran his fingers through his hair and swore under his breath as he turned and took in the damage.

"I'd better get out there and see if I can patch up that hole or else being in here won't be any better than standing in the storm."

Natalie nodded again, wondering how long it was going to take to regain control of her vocal cords.

DAMN IT ALL TO HELL.

Dan pulled on his jacket and headed out into a storm that had not diminished in strength. Spike followed, and he didn't have the energy or the conviction to tell the old dog to stay behind. Dan had barely slept last night, both the pain of his back on the hard cot and the pain of his memories making sleep all but impossible. When he had finally drifted off, his mind had been filled with images of the lady doc lying soft and warm beneath him.

He'd gotten up with the clear intention of getting them off this damn island and back to reality as soon as humanly possible.

But before he knew it, he was holding Natalie in his arms and thinking about how good, almost right, she felt there.

He slammed the door behind him, the violent storm whipping and pulling at him and doing little to combat his aroused state. Had Natalie noticed?

There had been a moment, a brief, sweet moment, when he'd been tempted to bend his head to hers and take a taste of those plump lips. When he'd looked deep into her eyes and felt as if his skin was on fire with the need to make love to her.

Thankfully, he'd come to his senses before he had kissed her. Lord only knew what she'd make of a simple kiss. What *he'd* make of a simple kiss. Hell, he was having a hard enough time merely thinking about kissing her.

The coast guard station was built against a ninety-degree incline, not unlike the houses on Courage Bay Mountain that had been so devastatingly affected by the mudslide. But here, decades-old trees still thrived, making the ground around them stable and solid, whereas land developers had stripped the mountain of much of the original vegetation to make room for the exclusive subdivision.

Dan zipped the jacket up to his chin and bent his head as he went down the stairs and rounded the raised structure, immediately seeing the cause of the cave-in. A large branch from a nearby pine must have been snapped off by the battering wind and rain, sending it crashing through the roof.

It was going to take a crane to remove it. Or at least more power than his two hands could provide.

No, he would have to find some way to keep the elements out, and leave the repairs to professionals.

He headed to the shed, where he'd seen a couple of boat tarps and a few two-by-fours stacked. Spike took care of his business under a nearby tree before following after him.

What the hell was it about Dr. Natalie Giroux that intrigued him so? Dan wondered. Made him want to kiss her when he had no intention of becoming romantically involved with anyone, especially not her?

He supposed their isolation was partially to blame. Hell, majorly to blame. Although he'd felt an attraction for her from the moment their eyes first met, in the usual day-to-day grind it was easy enough to avoid running into her. Which eliminated temptation altogether.

But here, alone with her on this deserted island, it seemed all he could do was think about her, and his want of her was growing exponentially with each moment that passed.

He hauled open the shed door and ducked inside, the wind threatening to rip the wooden barrier from its hinges. Mentally he calculated what it would take to patch up the hole. He'd have to make at least three trips to get the materials he needed out to the roof. Looking around for the tarps, he felt a moment's pause when he didn't find them where he expected to. Instead, there was only one tarp, and it was on the floor in the opposite corner of the shed. Strange...

A shadow fell over the entryway. Thinking the wind had blown the door partway closed, he turned...only to find Natalie standing there in her hooded slicker, patting Spike.

"Looks like you could use some help," she shouted over the banshee wind.

"I've got it!" he called back. "Go into the cabin. You're getting all wet."

One of her brows cocked up and Dan cringed.

"I think I've already proved to us both that I won't melt."

No, maybe she wouldn't. But just being around her, no matter the circumstances, made him feel as if something was melting inside of him. Something he wanted to keep intact.

He picked up the tarp and shoved it into her arms. She stumbled back a couple of steps from the unexpected weight, the wind nearly toppling her.

"Can you handle it?" he asked.

Her face was drawn into soft lines of concentration as she nodded and moved in the direction of the station.

Dan cursed under his breath. Damn woman. Being outside in the elements had been his only means of escape. Now even that had been snatched from him.

He jerkily piled the two-by-fours into his arms, determined to get this over in one trip. The sooner the roof was fixed, the sooner she could go back into the station and he could be by himself again. Where he could reerect the barriers that had deteriorated both last night and this morning. When he looked at Natalie, he didn't want to see a woman who'd worked hard to achieve her goal of being a burn specialist. He didn't want to think of the fiancé she'd lost or empathize with what she had gone through. He didn't want to think about asking her if she wanted children, or what her favorite color was, or if she was a morning person or a night owl. For just as his physical desire for her was growing, so was his curiosity. He felt an inexplicable need to know Dr. Natalie Giroux as intimately as possible. And that, most of all, puzzled him beyond reason.

"Stay off to the side!" he shouted when he'd climbed the incline next to the station and found her standing on the roof.

She glared at him as if to say she knew what she was doing, the cold rain having no effect on her heated stare.

Grabbing two corners of the tarp, she lifted it up to shake it, but the wind saw to the task for her, nearly blowing her right toward the jagged opening filled by the tree branch. Dan was too far away to do anything but watch helplessly as she regained her balance, Spike acting as a retaining wall as he stepped in front of her. Dan caught the other side of the tarp and positioned it over the two-foot-wide hole and the branch, immediately anchoring it with a two-by-four and kneeling to nail the wood in place. He finished and handed another two-by-four to Natalie, who repeated his actions on the other side.

"I can handle the rest," he shouted. "Why don't you take Spike and go back inside?"

Her grimace did funny things to his stomach.

"No sense in all of us getting wet," he added.

Of course, she didn't need to point out that she and Spike were already wet, probably soaked to the skin, but Dan wanted her out of his sight, and quickly. The raindrops clinging to her thick lashes made her eyes all the more intensely beautiful. And the way the drops slid over the rim of her bottom lip made him want to press his mouth against them, catch them with his tongue.

He very definitely needed her to get out of there…now.

Without saying another word, Natalie turned on her heel and made her way back into the station, Spike following her.

Dan's shoulders instantly relaxed with relief.

The problem was, he knew how very short-lived that relief would be. Because all too soon he would be trapped with her inside again….

CHAPTER NINE

NATALIE DID WHAT SHE could inside the coast guard station to keep busy. She was so restless she felt an inch away from jumping out of her skin. But mostly she didn't want to think about Dan and her reaction to being in his arms such a short time ago.

Of course, most women would probably be thinking about how close they'd come to being beaned in the head by a pine tree. But all that filled her mind was the image of Dan's passion-filled blue eyes and how very close his mouth had been to hers. All it would have taken was the tiniest of moves and she would have been kissing him.

If he had let her.

She vigorously rubbed her arms. Was it her imagination, or was he going out of his way to avoid her?

No, she wasn't that inventive. Dan was definitely steering clear of her. And she guessed the reason had little to do with his burn.

Then again, perhaps it had everything to do with it. After all, she hadn't exactly been the epitome of charm and grace when she'd shown up at the fire station and essentially demanded he disrobe right there on the spot so she could close the file on him. It didn't matter that she'd gone there as a favor to Debra. When Natalie was anywhere within a five-foot radius of Dan, her bedside manner flew straight out the window.

Her mind snagged on the word *bedside* and she quietly cleared her throat.

Instead of exploring the myriad reasons why she shouldn't link the words *bed* and *Dan* in the same sentence, she methodically cleared the debris off her cot, then swept and mopped the rest from the floor. When she was done, she gazed up at the pine branch. It looked oddly like an upside-down Christmas tree. The realization that the holiday was just next month caught her up short.

She moved back until her legs hit the side of Dan's cot. Slowly she sat down, her hands absently brushing over the taut canvas as she stared at the tree limb.

For the past year she'd purposely kept herself so busy she wouldn't have time to think about the devastated state of her personal life. Holidays came and went. While her brothers and her niece and nephew—Alec's children—wouldn't allow her complete escape into her work, she did manage to spend a great deal of her time at the hospital.

She hadn't even thought of what she might buy for

Stacy and Cameron. Then there were her brothers, whom she'd always had trouble buying for.

But that didn't really matter. They'd be happy with a homemade Christmas card. What bothered her was that when it came to her life, nothing much had changed since last Christmas. She seemed stuck in the past, unable to move forward.

It was said that everything got better with time.

She was coming to believe that was so much malarkey.

When she caught herself clutching the blanket Dan had used the night before, she slowly withdrew her hand and rose from the cot.

She cleaned out the bucket and mop in the tiny bathroom, washed up herself, then stepped out into the main cabin area. What was it about her that Dan found so unappealing? She glanced down at the borrowed pants and the blouse she'd had on yesterday, which had dried out enough for her to wear. Her brothers had always teased her about being on the thin side. But she couldn't help that. She'd always had to be reminded when to eat even when she was a kid.

Speaking of which…

She crouched down and went through the cupboard. That's funny. She could have sworn there'd been more cans of corned beef and soup in there when she'd first looked.…

She moved the cans around, then checked the cupboards to the left and right before coming back to the one she crouched in front of. It had been dark last night, so she hadn't gotten a good look, but she was fairly convinced the cupboard had been better stocked. Had Dan removed a few cans and put them somewhere else? But that didn't make sense.

Shaking her head, she took out one of the cans of corned beef and put it on the counter. Spike immediately understood that he was about to be fed, and nudged her knee with his nose. She smiled and patted him. "What's the matter, boy? Are you hungry?"

Once she'd scooped out the meat onto the same plate she'd used the night before, she retrieved the bowl of water she'd left for Spike and refilled it, then placed both food and water near the rug that doubled as the dog's bed. In no time flat the corned beef was history and Spike was looking at her, his tail going a million miles a minute.

Natalie had never had a pet before, so she didn't know if the food was enough to sustain him. But there were only two cans of corned beef left, and since she didn't know how long they would be stuck on the island, she figured it would be a good idea to err on the side of caution. Better to have too little now than to run out of food before they were rescued.

Her lips twisted in a wry smile. That probably went for her and Dan, as well. She knelt down and looked at the small stock of soup, making a mental note of what was there. Then she got to her feet and started going through the drawers. She spotted a deck of playing cards, which she took out and tossed onto the table. Then she made herself a cup of coffee, taking it easy on the cream and sugar lest it should run out before they got off this blasted island.

Some might find the prospect of being alone on a deserted island with a man like Dan Egan the things of which romance novels were made.

Natalie was finding it hell on earth.

She stared at the ceiling. The pounding had stopped an hour ago. Just where in the heck was Dan, anyway?

Her gaze drifted to the radio in the corner.

As if on cue, she heard the hum of the generator, and a moment later the overhead light flickered on.

It looked as if she and Dan were on the same wavelength. Which was fine with her. The sooner they were back on the mainland and well away from each other, the better for both of them.

But if she truly believed that, why did she feel a little thrill at the knowledge that he'd soon be back inside?

DAN HURRIED BACK INTO the cabin, shrugged out of his windbreaker and dried himself off slightly before heading straight for the communications radio. To his disappointment, Natalie was sitting in front of it, talking to Godfrey.

He stopped in the middle of the cabin, distantly aware that he was dripping water all over the floor, but unable to bring himself to care.

All he had to do was catch a glimpse of the woman and his stomach felt funny and he grew warm all over. He was getting the feeling that no matter how long he stayed out in the raging storm, that wouldn't change.

"Any good news you can share, God?" Natalie was asking, apparently already on a first-name basis with the ham radio operator they had been in contact with the night before.

"'Fraid not, Miss Natalie. NWS is reporting this system is parked over the area and not showing any signs of moving on."

Natalie glanced up at Dan. He ignored her and held the transmit mike up to his mouth, reintroducing himself. "Did you get our messages through to CBFD?"

"Yes, Dan, I did. I also spoke with the coast guard. They said that you're to sit tight. They'll get someone out there as soon as they can."

Dan dropped his chin to his chest and let out a long breath. At least he could rest assured that someone from the station had contacted Debra to let her know he was okay. He no longer had to worry about her worrying about him.

As for the mudslide, his men—and women—were well trained to take care of the situation on their own. If they weren't, they wouldn't be on his team.

Godfrey filled them in on power outages and additional mudslides in the area, then Dan ended the transmission and shut the radio down.

"Are you going back out?"

He glanced at Natalie, still seated on the radio stool. He'd had to bend over her left shoulder in order to speak to Godfrey, and hadn't moved since shutting off the radio.

This close, he could make out flecks of gold in her brown eyes, and a spattering of light freckles across her nose that gave her an almost girlish look. Although there was nothing else girlish about the provocative woman. And he'd be damned if her hair didn't still smell of lemons.

It would be so easy to lessen the distance between them and see if she tasted like the pungent fruit.

Only he didn't have to lessen the distance, because she already had.

Dan nearly groaned at the first contact of her warm mouth against his. He'd never considered the possibility that Natalie would take control. He'd assumed this battle was his own. She was showing him how off the mark he was, and he was helpless to stop her.

It seemed as if he'd been both waiting for and dreading this moment for longer than a day. And in all honesty, he had. He'd been wanting to kiss the capable and sexy Dr. Giroux ever since the first moment he'd laid eyes on her. And she didn't taste like lemons.

She tasted like coffee. And cream. And sugar. And a flavor uniquely hers.

He watched as her eyelids drooped down, inspiring him to slide his tongue past her soft lips and into the hot, honeyed recesses of her mouth.

Natalie's eyes closed completely, leaving him looking at the thick fringe of dark lashes against her cheeks as he threaded his fingers through her silken curls and pressed her mouth harder against his.

Damn, he'd instinctively known that kissing her would feel like heaven. And he'd also known she would be wonderfully warm and responsive, despite her abrasive manner. Beneath her bristly, professional exterior lay an inherently sensual woman who would drive any man mad with desire.

Lightly he grasped her shoulders, lifting her from the stool and kicking it away without breaking the contact of their mouths. She easily followed his lead, stepping flush against him. He felt her breasts press against his chest, her hips meet his, and knew an arousal so complete he burned with it.

Natalie's breath seemed to exit her lips on a sigh, making her almost completely boneless against him. Dan easily supported her weight even as her fingers dived under the back of his T-shirt and touched his bare skin. He shuddered with longing. It had been much, much too long since he'd known the beauty of such a simple touch. He'd thought that only Eleanor could ignite such a reaction in him.

He'd been wrong.

Dan waited for guilt to hit him—the overwhelming sensation that he'd somehow betrayed his wife's memory by admitting how much he wanted the woman in his arms. Instead he felt nothing but the trip of his heartbeat, the warmth of Natalie's body and a need so complete it nearly knocked his knees out from under him.

He moved his hand from her shoulder, running it ever so slowly toward her breasts. When he cupped one of the soft mounds of flesh, his temperature shot straight up into the danger zone and the slow, leisurely pace of their kissing picked up.

Then Natalie's fingers slid up his side and around to his back, touching the puckered skin of his burn scar.

They both froze.

Dan wasn't sure who was more surprised, him or her. For one brief moment they'd forgotten the roles they'd played in each other's lives, doctor and patient.

And he'd forgotten that he had no intention of letting her examine him.

Gently he pulled away, looking everywhere but at her.

"I, um, had better go shut down the generator," he said, his voice gravelly, reflecting the conflicting emotions burning through him.

Natalie quietly cleared her throat. "I knew you'd say that."

Despite Dan's best intentions, he met her gaze—and found slight amusement mingling with clear desire instead of the accusatory stare he'd grown used to.

Whoa.

He moved toward the door as fast as he could, away from this woman and her captivating charms.

AN HOUR LATER Dan was no closer to regaining control over his rampant hormones than he'd been before. If anything, the thundering need within him to claim Natalie in an even more intimate way had increased, making his blood thick with desire, his every move lethargic.

He'd put off returning to the station for as long as he could. He'd checked the tarp, secured the shed door, retied the rope anchoring the chopper in place, and now found himself standing at the foot of the station stairs, staring up dubiously.

A strange rattling captured his attention. He looked to his right, where a two-foot-square sheet of fiberglass was being battered against the lower bows of a pine tree. Bending into the wind, he crossed to peel the material from the tree. *SS Minnow IV* was written in large blue letters. Debris from a boat?

He glanced up the beach to his right, knowing

there was nothing to his left, in the direction of the chopper, or he would have seen it before now. As soon as he'd anchored the piece of fiberglass where it couldn't cause any damage, he headed north along the beach. A couple hundred yards up, he spotted it. A small, single-engine fishing boat, battered beyond repair, sat against the fringe of the forest. It was turned on its side, the cracked bottom facing the bay. Dan examined both the boat and the area around it, but saw nothing to indicate anyone had washed ashore with the light craft.

Lightning struck overhead and he winced as he scanned the beach, then called out to see if anyone was around. There was no response. He'd turned to head back toward the station when his foot caught on something metal, partially covered by wet sand. Bending over, he wiped it off and found it was a red, ten-gallon gasoline can—empty, he discovered when he'd pulled it free.

Minutes later Dan stood inside the door to the station, dripping a puddle around his feet.

Natalie looked up from where she was playing solitaire at the table, which she had moved against the front wall. For better light, he guessed.

He searched her face for any clue that might tell him how she felt about what had passed between them, but he found nothing.

Dan shrugged out of his jacket and slipped off his

shoes, then headed for the small washroom. A short time later, in fresh clothes and with a mug of coffee, he felt marginally drier, but no better. All he could seem to do was look at Natalie's eyes and remember how inviting they had been just before he'd kissed her. Stare at her lips and think about how damn good they had felt against his. Gaze at the front of her blouse and imagine the imprint of her breast against his palm.

"Hungry?" she asked, disturbing the silence.

Dan took a long pull from his mug, then shook his head. "You?"

She counted another three cards and turned them over before shaking her own head.

He supposed they really should put something into their stomachs. It was after noon and neither of them had had anything more than the watery soup the night before. But somehow he didn't think he could force anything down his tight throat. It was hard enough drinking the coffee.

Natalie had been busy in the station, he noticed now. She'd trimmed off the smaller branches of the huge tree limb that had crashed through the roof, cleaned up the debris and put the cots and blankets away. If not for the branch poking through the roof, the only way someone could tell they'd been there was that the place was cleaner than before.

And, of course, minus a few food supplies.

He squinted at the branch. Was it his imagination or were there little straw bows tied to some of the remaining twigs? He drew nearer and realized she'd used twine.

Natalie cleared her throat.

Dan rounded the table and turned a chair around, straddling it backward. "Tell me you didn't decorate the tree?"

Keeping her attention on her game, Natalie lightly shrugged. "Then I won't."

Despite himself, Dan cracked a smile.

Only Natalie Giroux, stranded in a cabin in the middle of a storm, would think to decorate a tree limb that had crashed through the roof.

Actually, that really wasn't a true assessment. Dan would never have guessed she'd do something so…sentimental. From what he'd seen so far, she was a no-nonsense type of woman who put her career well before house and hearth.

Why, then, the bows on the branch?

He squinted at her in the dim light. It seemed there was much more to the lady doc than he'd suspected. And while their conversations since being stranded the day before had revealed a little more about her, he still didn't know what made her tick. What was it she held in her heart? What did she secretly wish for above all else?

"Are you just going to sit there staring at me all

afternoon?" she asked quietly, jarring him from his thoughts.

He put his mug down on the table. "I was thinking about it."

She gathered the cards together and began shuffling. "You know it's highly rude to stare, don't you?"

Dan crossed his arms on the back of the chair and aimed his best Texas grin her way. "If you're asking if my mama taught me any manners, why, yes, ma'am, she did."

Laughter flared in Natalie's mocha eyes. "I keep forgetting you're a Texan."

"You say that like I'm from another planet or something."

She put the cards down. "You might as well be."

"Have you ever been to Texas?"

"Aside from an extended residency in Cleveland, I haven't been more than an hour outside Courage Bay."

Dan cocked a brow. His career in the military and then in the fire department had taken him pretty much all over, including places outside the States. "That's a shame. Texas has a lot to offer."

Her gaze traveled over his T-shirt-covered torso. "I bet."

Casually he reached for the deck of cards, even though his desire had spiked right back up to high. His fingers brushed against hers and he could swear he felt her shiver. "You play poker?" he asked.

"Is that a Texas thing?"

He shook his head as he shuffled. "But I have heard it said that the game was invented there."

She laughed at that, as he'd intended her to. "So long as the type of poker you have in mind doesn't have the word *strip* in there anywhere, I'm game."

Dan's throat nearly closed off altogether as images of Natalie slipping out of her blouse, sexily revealing her pale flesh, crowded his mind, almost causing him to drop the cards.

"Okay, then. How about we start off slow…?"

CHAPTER TEN

THREE HOURS LATER Dan was having a hard time concentrating on the game. Not because Natalie was beating the pants off him—figuratively, because as promised, he'd kept "strip" out of the poker, no matter how much he wanted to do otherwise. But sitting across from her and not being able to touch her was wreaking havoc on his willpower.

"I'm getting the distinct impression you've played this game before," he said dryly.

She smiled as she gathered the cards and began shuffling them like a pro. "You forget I was raised with two brothers."

"Mmm. Yes, I guess I did forget." He waggled a finger at her. "But that doesn't change the fact that your silence when I asked if you played indicated that you didn't."

"My mistake."

Her cheeks were flushed, the dim light from the window and from a single oil lamp enhancing rather than detracting from her natural beauty.

And it was natural. Given their circumstances, he'd have found it highly strange had she tried to do something with her hair, or put on makeup. Thankfully, she'd done neither, beyond running a comb through her curly dark tresses and brushing her teeth. Although the fact she carried a toothbrush and paste in her purse warned that she might be a little on the anal side, even for a doctor. But, hey, there were far worse things. Like seeing a compact as more important than a toothbrush. She hadn't even bothered with lipstick, but the natural deep raspberry color of her lips made remembering how they tasted all too easy.

"Another go, or should we break for a late lunch, early dinner?" she asked now.

"Break," he said. "I don't know if I can stand the abuse without some grub in my stomach."

They both got up and stepped to the counter at the back, where they worked together until soup was in mugs and the crackers on the table between them. Their actions were so domestic and so in sync, Dan thought. Instinctively, each seemed to know what the other needed. He reached to get a spoon to stir the soup; she handed him one without his asking. She took the glass chimney off a second lantern and he was ready with the matches to light it.

While he knew his way around a kitchen—life at a fire station demanded that everyone pitch in—he'd never spent much time in his own kitchen at home beyond pouring himself some coffee and getting out the cinnamon rolls Debra had dropped off the night before for breakfast. And it was only after Eleanor died that he began doing that. His late wife had looked after everything for him.

Had he ever fixed a meal in his own house? The thought caught him up short. Had he ever given his wife breakfast in bed?

With surprise, he realized the idea to cook breakfast or any other meal had never occurred to him. His and Ellie's roles had been so clearly defined that him cooking at home would have been as shocking as Ellie showing up at the station and wanting to go out on a run.

Even when his wife was ill, Debra, Ellie's family and the neighbors had seen to all of the cooking and household chores.

"Penny for your thoughts," Natalie said.

Dan was momentarily startled, both by his reflections and her softly spoken words.

He gave her one of his best grins. "Is that all my thoughts are worth?"

She sat back in her chair, warming her hands around her mug, apparently waiting for the soup to cool before drinking it. "Name your price then."

He shook his head. "Nothing."

One of her finely shaped brows rose behind her fringe of bangs.

"Not my price. What I mean is that I wasn't thinking at all. Not really."

Untrue, but if he'd learned anything during twenty years of marriage, it was that in some cases, little white lies were not only permissible but downright necessary. He didn't want Natalie to believe he thought about his late wife every moment of every day. It sounded…odd.

And, he realized, it was odd.

Was it normal that two years after Ellie's death he was rummaging through the past, looking for answers that couldn't be found? What would Natalie think if she knew he still half expected to get up in the morning and find Ellie turning eggs in the kitchen? Or that he still kept her perfume in his sock drawer and every now and again took it out and sniffed it, trying to recapture a moment long gone?

Although lately, he admitted, the incidences happened less and less frequently. It was only now, sharing a cabin with Natalie, that his past with Ellie seemed to occupy so much of his thoughts.

He stared at the soup in his cup.

"What will you give me for *my* thoughts, then?" Natalie asked.

Dan squinted at her. "Hmm?"

Her smile tightened the knot in his stomach. "My thoughts. How much will you give me for them?"

So preoccupied with his own private musings, Dan couldn't think of a way to respond.

"Okay, how about I offer them up for free? You know, just this once? Consider it a sample against future purchases."

Dan smiled.

She sat back and crossed her legs. The action shouldn't have been sexy, but it was to Dan. "I was just thinking how much more...relaxed you looked this afternoon," she said, dipping her spoon into the mug and stirring.

"How do you mean?"

Her casual shrug drew his attention to the soft cotton of her T-shirt and the way the material draped over her breasts. "I don't know. When we first got here yesterday and had pretty much figured out we were stuck for the duration of the storm...well, you looked like you wished you were anywhere in the world but here...with me."

That about summed up his feelings. "Go on," he said.

She made a face, then tested the soup, apparently judging it still too hot, since she blew on it. She looked up at him. "Is that how you felt?"

Dan gave her a half smile as he slowly sipped from his mug. "I was under the impression it was your thoughts we were sharing."

She tilted her head slightly, considering him. "It was, wasn't it? The way you felt, I mean."

He didn't answer. Part of those manners his

mother had taught him included not saying anything at all if he didn't have anything nice to say.

"Don't worry. I wasn't thrilled about being stuck here with you, either."

Dan hiked his brows at this. "Oh?"

Her smile was decidedly sheepish. "Would you like me to outline why?"

Her reasons rated an entire outline?

He put his mug down and righted his chair. "By all means, go ahead."

She had watched his movements closely and now shifted her gaze back to his face. "Okay. Just remember you asked for it."

Although Dan couldn't recall asking her for anything, he wasn't going to argue the point. He was too busy enjoying the animated expression on her face as she mentally readied her thoughts.

"First, the last thing on my agenda yesterday was tracking you down at the fire station so I could perform a follow-up examination that should have happened three months ago."

Even now Dan sat slightly to one side so the chair back didn't put any pressure on his burn scar. But he wasn't about to share that bit of information with her.

"I mean, I'm not averse to making house calls. I do it all the time for elderly patients and young children. But since you don't fall into either category…"

"Oh, I don't know. I think some might say I fall into the former one."

She looked surprised by his response.

"Anyway, continue," he said, uncomfortable with what he might have revealed with his comment.

"Okay," she said slowly, apparently trying to find her way back to where she'd left off. "So I agree to make this special firehouse call as a favor to a friend—your daughter, Debra—and once I get there, I catch grief from you for tracking you down, even though you were the one who was a no-show five times. Do you know how many other patients I could have seen, rather than sitting around waiting for you to show up?"

He decided the lady doc was more than a little pretty when she got all worked up.

"Then the mudslide happens...."

She glanced around the coast guard station. She didn't need to go into detail about the circumstances surrounding their current predicament. They both knew them well.

Natalie crossed her slender arms on the table and leveled a stare at him. "You're pigheaded, do you know that?"

Dan wasn't quite sure where that one had come from. "Pardon me?"

"You heard me," she whispered, looking a little more emotional than the conversation warranted. Her eyes seemed overly bright. And he suspected it was pain—induced by something internal rather than external—that was behind the pinched skin between her brows. "You're stubborn. And you think pride is never having to rely on others, even when what you're doing is just plain stupid."

This was definitely not what Dan had signed up for. He'd expected her to tell him he'd been rude. Not the best of shack-buddies. But never would he have anticipated this.

"There's a man I used to know who was exactly like you. Only because of his own stupid pride, he's dead now."

Oh, boy.

Dan watched as she sat back in her chair, grasping her mug tightly in white fingers. A lone tear rolled over her lower lashes and down her cheek. Not that Natalie appeared to notice. Her concentration seemed fixed on her hands and the contents of the mug she held.

Her voice was so soft that Dan barely made it out over the roar of the storm beyond the window next to them. "Charles...well, he refused to listen to the warning signs his body was sending him. I made him two appointments with a cardiologist at the hospital, but he missed both of them. If he had gone to just one..."

This wasn't about him, Dan realized. This was about her late fiancé, and he just happened to be around to take the abuse.

Or was this about him?

Absently he rubbed his eyebrows. "Are you saying I could die from the burn scar?"

The question sounded dumb to his own ears.

Until she blinked up at him. "Yes."

NATALIE HELD DAN'S WARY gaze.

She hadn't really meant to imply that he could drop dead right there on the spot. And she hadn't intended to alarm him.

Or maybe she had.

Either way, she'd gotten the response she'd been looking for. He appeared shocked and concerned. And he was finally paying attention to her. As well he should be.

No, the burn wouldn't find him in the hospital tomorrow, fighting for his life. But the long-term effects could impact the quality of his life and possibly shorten it if he wasn't careful.

But she wasn't going to explain that part to him. She had his attention. That was what mattered to her now.

"Given our close proximity, I've been able to observe you, Dan," she said, regaining control over her runaway emotions and surprised to find her cheeks damp. "I can tell the wound is causing you problems. The key word being *wound*. Not scar, as you put it."

"But three months have passed since the warehouse fire. Surely the wound's healed by now."

"If that's the case, then why do you wince every time you do something that stretches that area? Why are you even now sitting in a way that guarantees that side isn't touching the chair?"

She watched as he shifted, the resulting wince clearly evident.

"Tell me, would you send someone you pulled off the street with no prior training in to fight a four-alarm fire?" she asked.

He appeared affronted. "Are you trying to tell me that I'm unqualified to recognize the messages my own body is sending me?"

"I'm saying I've trained for years to do my job. Why don't you let me do it?"

For long moments there was nothing but the sound of the fierce storm outside the station, the wind whipping at the tarp they'd placed over the collapsed roof. Natalie thought she'd just set everything between them back the way it was the previous day. But she couldn't help herself. Watching him sit there, blatantly refusing to admit he was in pain, bared an emotional wound within her. Her trauma might not be as fresh, as evident, but it was no less severe.

How many times had she sat across from Charles, watching as he absently rubbed his left arm? Paused so he could catch his breath during a walk through the park, when she was barely winded? Watched him flinch and clutch his chest, then play it off as nothing more than indigestion as a result of the chili she'd cooked for dinner?

Too many times. And every time she'd felt an odd foreboding.

In retrospect, she'd clearly seen what was coming, even if she couldn't guess at the devastating consequences. Ultimately she'd been as passive as he was in allowing it to happen. She may have made the medical appointments for him, but perhaps she could have been more diligent about seeing he got to them.

"You can lead a horse to water but you can't make him drink," Dan said quietly.

Natalie blinked at him. She hadn't said what she was thinking aloud, had she? No, she hadn't.

He softly smiled at her. "That's what my wife used to say. My late wife, I mean."

Natalie looked down at the ring he still wore, which from time to time she caught him nudging around his thick finger.

"You asked if anyone told me I was pigheaded before. Strange you should choose that word, because that's exactly what Ellie used to call me. Debra, too."

Though she felt compelled to smile back at him, Natalie restrained herself. She couldn't lessen the pressure on him. She needed to get a look at that burn.

"I thought they were just being nags. You know, behaving in that way women do in order to get what they want. Only in this case, maybe you and Debra are right."

He got up, turned his chair around and pulled his T-shirt off. "She's all yours, Doc."

CHAPTER ELEVEN

THE DAMP AIR WAS COOL against Dan's back as he stiffly sat in the hard wooden chair, waiting for Natalie to react to what he'd said.

Instead she sat staring at him from across the table as if he'd asked her to clean up Spike's mess after he'd gotten into a bag of prunes.

"I don't get it—I thought this was what you wanted," he said quietly.

She nodded. "It is...."

"But?"

She shook her head and he guessed she really wasn't seeing him. "It's just that…"

Dan squinted at her. Women. He'd never be able to figure them out.

"Five seconds and the shirt goes back on," he said, giving her fair warning.

After all, a guy could be patient for only so long. Especially when it came to wounds and doctors. Especially his wounds and this particular lady doctor.

The scent of lemons assaulted his senses as she

slowly rounded the table and stood behind him.
While he could no longer see her, he was aware of
her presence in a way he'd never been aware of anyone's before. In a way that had nothing to do with
burns or doctors, and everything to do with what
happened between a man and a woman.

He'd once wholeheartedly believed that he'd been
too lucky the first time around. That his marriage and
years with Eleanor were more than one man deserved
in a lifetime. But his burgeoning feelings for Natalie
were making him think perhaps he'd been ten kinds
of a fool. No matter what he said, no matter what he
did, he couldn't seem to shake his interest in her.

He heard her soft intake of breath and stiffened
further.

"Oh, Dan, what have you done?" she whispered,
but he knew she really wasn't expecting an answer.
"It's worse than I thought."

Dan gripped the chair back a little tighter but otherwise didn't indicate any concern at what she was
saying, even though he was thoroughly alarmed.

He felt her fingertips on the outer fringes of the
burn and swallowed hard. Despite everything, her
touch was doing strange things to his stomach that
had nothing to do with pain and too much to do with
pleasure.

"You see, when you first came in, the destroyed
epidermis was still present and the blistering was so

bad that I couldn't get a good look, determine how deep the wound went, no matter how much I cleaned it up. That's why I asked you to come back the following day so I could further wash away and debride the dead skin and better diagnose the wound—see what needed to be done."

Her touch moved across the burn area and he winced. He didn't like her connecting the word *dead* to anything having to do with him.

"This goes much deeper than even I could have imagined. Dan, I suspect you have major muscle damage here, and probably some nerve damage, as well."

From a damn burn?

He was growing increasingly concerned.

"Have you been exercising?"

Dan grimaced. What did that have to do with his wound? "I've been known to lift a few weights."

"That's what I thought. You see, if you'd come back, I would have been able to debride a lot of the burned skin that's now permanently dead, excise a great deal of the rest, and graft living tissue to the wound. I would also have scheduled you some time with a physical therapist, who would have given you a series of exercises to do every day so your skin, muscles and nerves could heal properly. What you've done…well, it's no wonder your range of motion is impaired."

"Nothing about me is impaired."

She laughed quietly. "You're right. At least physically. Mentally…" She poked around some more, causing him to jerk. "I guess the word I was looking for was *limited*. By not coming back the next day…by not taking the steps necessary for your wound to heal properly…you've made it worse."

Dan's muscles were taut, her every touch, every soft breath pulling them tighter and tighter.

The way he saw it, his desire to kiss Natalie was quickly pushing aside his concern for his wound and what he had and hadn't done, and causing him to focus instead on what he'd rather be doing.

In one smooth move—and despite the pain that shot through him—he slid back in the chair, grasped her arm and pulled her into his lap.

Her breathless gasp touched off a series of sensations deep in his stomach.

"There's also nothing limited about my range of motion," he murmured, his words lacking the conviction he'd intended to put into them.

Now that he had her in his lap, her bottom hot against him, her arms linked around his neck to steady herself, her subtle scent overwhelming his senses, everything about him shifted a little off center.

During the past few months, he'd vehemently fought his attraction to her. But in only two days, he'd discovered that the differences he'd stacked up between them in an effort to keep away from her had been eliminated one by one.

And the important thing was this moment—when he had an opportunity to hold her in his arms. When his heart rate kicked up and his stomach twisted and his groin ached with the need to make love to her.

"So what's the prognosis, Doc?" he asked, his voice sounding rough and gravelly.

Her eyes darkened with desire as her gaze moved from his eyes to his lips, then back again. "Why don't we, um, talk about that later?"

He cocked a grin. "That bad?"

He watched a swallow work its way down the slender column of her throat. "Yes."

Maybe the word should have concerned him more. But he couldn't quite latch on to it. There were other things on his mind just then. Like how he was going to make love to Dr. Natalie Giroux without the roof caving in on top of them.

NATALIE COULDN'T SEEM TO pull in a deep breath as she stared up into Dan's strikingly handsome face, made even more appealing by the undeniable desire burning there.

He wanted her. Oh, he might be able to hide it well enough when he was moving around, keeping busy, rushing out into the storm to see to one chore or another. But when she was in his arms, she felt his need for her so strongly it took her breath away.

Had things ever been this way between her and Charles? She couldn't seem to remember. The past twelve months had been filled with such pain and regret that it was almost impossible to recall anything before that.

All she knew was that what was happening between her and Dan was more than a case of runaway hormones. While the storm might be responsible for their being stranded together, what she was feeling was no momentary attraction brought about by circumstances.

"You can lead a horse to water, but you can't make him drink."

Dan's words came back to her and she applied the meaning to the two of them. While the storm had thrust them together, it hadn't brought them to this moment. They had. Their attraction for each other had begun long before she had been ready to admit it, intensifying over the past few months, fueled by a will of its own.

"Is it all right if I kiss you, Doc?"

Dan's words sent heat skittering all through her body. "I'd be highly offended if you didn't."

She caught his slight grin before he lowered his head to hers.

The first time they'd kissed had come as a shock to them both. But now... Now Natalie was expecting it, anticipating it. Still, she was wholly unprepared for the brushfire of desire that swept through her at the mere touch of his lips against hers.

Dan was large and powerful and two hundred percent male. Everything about him spoke of a man capable of any task set before him, a man completely in charge. He was driven by instinct, while so much of Natalie's life had been based on reason and logic. But the strong emotions surging through her now were foreign and frightening, and utterly irresistible.

Since he'd lain on the emergency room table three months ago, there had been a few times late into the night when she'd considered the man with the intense gaze, and thought that any woman wanting to be with him would be required to give up control in order to do so. Of course, since control meant so much to her, had been such a large part of her life, that made him immediately off-limits.

Now, as she hungrily explored his mouth while he was exploring hers, she wondered if there had to be a giving up of control at all. Perhaps they could share it.

Natalie lifted her hands from behind his neck and threaded her fingers through his thick, dark hair. He tasted so good, making her hungry for more. She reveled in the texture of his tongue against hers, the smooth ridges of his teeth, the firm feel of his lips.

He slowly slid his hand under the hem of her wrinkled blouse, the touch of his fingers against her bare skin chasing out whatever breath she held in her lungs. Her stomach twitched and her flesh tingled as he spread his fingers, as if the mere feel of her skin fascinated him. Finally he cupped her breast through her bra. Natalie shivered, molten heat washing over her in welcoming waves.

The fevered meeting of their mouths increased in intensity, until finally Dan broke free, resting his forehead against hers as they fought to catch their breath.

"I want to make love to you, Natalie."

She searched his eyes, her heart expanding in her chest and pressing against her rib cage. "Like I said before, I'd be highly offended if you didn't."

That appeared to be all the incentive Dan needed. He got up from the chair, taking her with him, and strode toward the storage closet and the blankets piled inside. Natalie could have suggested the process might go faster if he put her down, so she could help spread the blankets out, but other, more important things captured her attention. More specifically, kissing the side of his thickly corded neck.

Finally he lowered her onto what felt like a hundred wool blankets. Natalie was aware that the stress of his movements had to be causing him pain, but she knew better than to argue the point with him. Instead she lay back, watching as he undid the buttons of her blouse, slowly, deliberately, as if anticipation was half the fun. Finally he fanned open the flaps, revealing her bra underneath.

Natalie focused on breathing in and out, watching his face as he took her in. She'd never been comfortable with her own nudity. At the health club she didn't stay and shower with the other women, but instead headed back to her place in her sweaty clothes.

Did Dan approve of her body? Did he find her attractive?

He dragged his fingers up from her waist to cup both breasts in his big palms, and Natalie stopped thinking entirely. Her eyes fluttered closed as she gave herself over to the pure sensation of him touching her.

A little while later, after they had leisurely removed each other's clothing, Dan was cradled between her damp thighs, gazing down at her with an intensity that filled Natalie with an unnamable feeling.

"I don't have, um…"

She searched his face. He seemed out of sorts, almost baffled. Then she realized what he was trying to say.

"Protection?" she whispered.

He nodded slightly, looking relieved that she had provided the word for him.

Of course, neither of them would have condoms. Natalie suspected that Dan hadn't been with another woman since his wife's death two years ago. And she…

For long moments she merely stared into his eyes, so full of need for him that her heart ached.

Finally, she answered his unspoken question by skimming the backs of her fingers down the flat muscles of his abdomen. She gently grasped his length in her hand and guided him to where she so wanted him to be.

Dan closed his eyes and his jaw tightened as he entered her in one smooth, long stroke.

Natalie moaned as Dan filled her, his turgid arousal claiming her slick, soft flesh. Every part of her seemed unbearably alive as pressure built up in her womb. She moved her feet to the back of his calves and opened to him further.

He slowly withdrew, then filled her again, setting her on fire. She grasped his shoulders, hanging on to his finely sculpted muscles to brace herself as he stroked her again, then again, each time deeper than before. His movements were so painfully sweet she felt tears burn the backs of her eyelids. She moved her hands to his hips, then around to touch his buttocks. The next time he stroked her, she held him there with the gentle pressure of her hands and tilted her hips up, taking him in even farther.

He leaned down and kissed her just as the shivers working over her skin turned into all-out convulsions of exquisite pleasure, and his own body stiffened in climax.

THE FIGURE ON THE OTHER side of the window stood in shadow, completely still despite the wind and rain assaulting him from behind. He watched the couple inside the warm cabin with curious detachment, finding the physical display not as interesting as the one he'd seen at producer Dylan Deeb's house yesterday. Then again, what was happening between the couple before him was consensual. What Dylan Deeb had done to the young blond actress in the middle of the day in his living room…well, he had seen the tears on the girl's face even as Deeb had directed her to disrobe and bend over the back of his expensive white leather sofa.

Of course, he'd been warm and dry himself, standing behind a bedroom door, caught off guard while burglarizing Deeb's house when the producer came home. A couple minutes later the actress had joined him.

He should have left then. But something had made him stay. Something about the look on Deeb's face as he talked to the actress told him something wasn't right. Only he could never have predicted what had happened next. He'd thought maybe the producer wanted to get a look at the girl's assets.

Instead the producer had taken full advantage and sampled the girl's wares, as well.

Then again, if he recalled correctly, Deeb had been arrested on similar charges six months ago.

Fire Chief Dan Egan looked toward the window,

and the man drifted farther back into the shadows. That's how he'd gotten caught earlier. Deeb had looked up while taking advantage of the actress, and stared right at him. He wasn't about to let that happen to him twice. Not when the first time had sent him on the run with his stolen items, a K-9 mutt chasing him all over Courage Bay Mountain before he finally decided the bay was his only means of escape.

The figure turned and descended the stairs, almost deafened by the sound of the waves crashing against the beach a few meters away. He was soaked to the skin. And he hadn't eaten anything but a can of soup and corned beef since yesterday. Still, his circumstances were a vast improvement over the experience of bobbing on the storm-tossed waves in the fishing boat he'd stolen. He'd fully expected the small craft to capsize.

Instead, the storm had slammed him against the shores of S-hamala Island. He'd just figured out he was alone when he'd heard the medevac helicopter above him, the chopper's engine cutting on and off, and knew he was going to have company. Which left the abandoned coast guard cabin off-limits to him. He'd constructed a lean-to inland with the help of some tarps and supplies he'd found in the shed. The fuel from the boat had helped ignite the wet wood he was able to gather for a warm fire.

It was his luck to be stuck on the island with Fire Chief Dan Egan.

Oh, he didn't know the guy, but he was familiar with him. Had seen his face in the paper again just the other day in connection with the warehouse explosion a few months back. The incident and the burns he'd sustained had made the photogenic fire chief front-page news for a week.

The only thing he had going for him was that the chief and his lady didn't seem to have a clue as to his presence. And his only hope of getting off this island a free man depended on the continuation of that state of affairs....

He hunched over in his raincoat and headed back toward his camp.

And if they did find out, he'd be wanted for far more than stealing a few things from wealthy people's homes...

A LONG TIME LATER, Dan lay on his good side with Natalie's soft body curled against his chest. Her shallow breathing told him she'd fallen asleep some minutes ago, but he refused to follow. He'd meant to pull out when he'd reached orgasm the first time, but when that moment arrived sooner than he'd anticipated, and Natalie held him close and moved her hips, he'd completely forgotten about his plans and had filled her with the hot proof of his need for her.

After that, there had been no reason for him to withdraw, so he hadn't.

He thought he heard a sound distinct from the now familiar white noise of wind and rain. His gaze snapped to the dark window, his every reflex on alert. He stared at the storm-swept night beyond for long minutes, but when he didn't detect anything unusual, he relaxed back into the blankets and considered the woman in his arms.

With his large fingers, he lightly brushed a few wispy bangs back from Natalie's forehead. How old was she? He'd initially thought her closer to forty than thirty, but now found himself questioning that assumption. At any rate, she was definitely still able to bear children.

The mere thought of possibly having impregnated her crowded his chest with all sorts of conflicting emotions.

He and Ellie had been blessed with only one child. A daughter. Debra. They'd never used protection, and had always hoped for more children, which had never come.

Now...

Now, well, he was too damn old to be tempting a visit from the stork again. Debra was nineteen years old, for God's sake. What would she have to say about having a sister or brother an entire generation younger than her? And when Debra married and had children of her own, would his grandchildren have an aunt or uncle their own age?

Dan ran his hand over his face, realizing that he needed a shave.

A shave? Hell, he needed to have his head examined.

He was just getting used to the idea of being attracted to the pushy doctor. Was he anywhere near ready to consider more?

Whatever gray light they'd had through the day had long since disappeared, leaving only the glow of the lantern. The soft light glinted on his wedding ring and he squeezed his eyes shut.

He'd spent the last two years living in the past. What in the hell did he know about the future?

He thought about getting up, going back out into the storm to check the chopper and the roof—something, anything other than lying here with Natalie as if everything was all right.

Gazing down at her face, he found her eyes open, quietly taking him in.

"What's wrong?" she asked.

Dan stared at her long and hard. Whatever his problems, Natalie deserved more than having him leave the makeshift bed right after making love to her. She deserved more than that. Deserved more than him.

He slowly shook his head and tried for a smile. "Nothing," he said, then leaned down and kissed her. "Go back to sleep."

She sighed softly and cuddled a little closer, making Dan want to just close his eyes and feel. If only for tonight. Tomorrow and its many problems would come soon enough.

CHAPTER TWELVE

DAN AWOKE WITH A START, his skin coated in sweat, his heart threatening to beat straight out of his chest. He jackknifed to a sitting position and ran his hand over his face, trying to clear his vision. The station. Blankets in the middle of the room. The fact that he wore nothing.

His gaze flew to the open bathroom door and Spike's empty rug. The dim light filling the room told him it was daytime. That the few minutes of shut-eye he had allowed himself last night had turned into a solid eight hours of sleep.

And his aching body told him he was much too old to be sleeping on the floor.

The sound of shouting came from outside.

Bolting to his feet, Dan grabbed his jeans and T-shirt and rushed to the door. He flung it open, allowing the elements to whip him at will as he dressed. Rain pelted his face, despite the porch over-hang, and wind tore at his clothing.

Eyes narrowed, he searched the storm-ravaged

beach for the source of the shout. Had Natalie taken Spike out and gotten lost in the storm? He could see the chopper, still secure, but no sign of woman or dog.

He turned in the opposite direction…and immediately made out what looked like a single-engine sailboat grounded on the rocky beach a couple hundred yards to the north.

Dan rushed down the stairs and over the debris-strewn sand toward the wreckage, barely aware of his bare feet, his lack of a jacket. The rain made his vision blurry, but he could see well enough to spot Natalie trying to pull the boat upright with the help of a young man no bigger than she was.

"Dan!" she shouted, her features instantly suffused with relief when she saw him, although she didn't loosen her grip on the boat. "Help us get this upright. The mast is pinned against his leg."

With one glance Dan took in the situation. A woman and a little girl no more than four or five stood huddled beneath a tree. Inside the sailboat, was a man somewhere around his own age, his left leg practically squashed under the thirty-foot mast, which must have come out of its mooring during the wreck.

Dan motioned toward the teenaged boy. "Come over to this side!"

The kid hesitated, then edged around the boat to join him.

"Grab the mast. No—no, more toward the top. That's it. As high as you can get. Nat?"

Natalie released her grip and came to stand next to him.

"Take the woman and the girl back to the cabin," he shouted over the howl of the wind.

She blinked against the rain running into her eyes. "What? You need my help here."

"Just do it!"

She stumbled back a couple of feet as if he'd struck her.

"I can be of more help out here."

Dan took a deep breath, reminding himself that Natalie wasn't one of his men, she was a stubborn, well-educated female. Barking orders wouldn't work. He'd have to reason with her. "What's your name, son?" he asked the teen.

"Jeremy. Jeremy Johnson."

"Trust me," Dan said, looking back at Natalie, "Jeremy and I can handle this. You can do more good by heading back to the station and getting ready for when we bring Mr. Johnson into the cabin."

"Mr. Moorhead," the boy corrected.

Dan blinked at him. He'd assumed the man was the youth's father. Obviously he'd been mistaken.

Natalie finally seemed to catch the logic of what he was saying, and nodded.

As she approached the woman and girl, Dan ordered Spike to follow her back to the station.

"Okay, on the count of three, I want you to push as hard as you can. You got that, Jeremy?"

AN HOUR LATER, with everyone safely inside the cabin, Natalie's blood still thrummed with the rush of adrenaline. Usually when she attended patients at the hospital, they'd already been through emergency and cleaned up. The ambulance didn't rush up to deliver a patient directly to her. As an E.R. attending physician, her brother Alec was in charge of that.

But in the past three days she'd been on the front lines of an emergency situation twice.

She looked across the room at the small family huddled together under blankets and drinking mugs of soup. Ken and Nessa Moorhead were on a cot, while the boy, Jeremy, and girl, little Trilby, sat on a blanket at their feet. Dan had fastened a temporary splint to Ken's leg after Natalie diagnosed it as broken. She'd drained a particularly nasty looking hematoma at the site of the contusion, then bandaged the area as best she could with the medical supplies Dan had collected from the downed chopper. It was obvious Ken was in a great deal of pain, but he kept it under wraps around his family, refusing the painkillers Natalie offered him.

She shivered. Although she'd changed into dry clothes, she still felt inexplicably chilled. She glanced over at Dan. He stood in front of the door like some kind of dark sentinel, and she knew her physical state was directly linked to the shift in his attitude to her from warm to coolly professional.

"I don't know what we would have done without you two," Nessa Moorhead said, gathering the soup mugs and bringing them to the sink, where Natalie stood. "We should never have taken the boat into the bay. We've been out there ever since the storm struck and…"

Three days. They'd been out on the storm-tossed waves of Courage Bay for three days. It was a miracle they were still alive.

Natalie stayed her with a hand to the shoulder, indicating she'd take care of dish duty. "Why don't you go over there with your family? They need you more than these mugs right now."

Nessa gave her a feeble smile, said thanks, then went back to the cot.

"I'm going to go restart the generator," Dan said, reaching for his windbreaker.

"Wait…" Natalie moved to join him at the door.

He stared down at her, his expression shuttered, his eyes devoid of emotion. Natalie wanted to hit him—a strange reaction for her.

"What's the matter, Dan?" she asked quietly. "Ever since we came inside, you've been acting…I guess *strange* would be the word."

He looked at her long and hard. "What were you doing out there by yourself?"

"Excuse me?"

He didn't say anything, merely waited for her response.

"I took Spike out and I happened to see the boat crash ashore. I was closer to them than I was to the station." She took in his defensive stance. "Look, Dan, this…your attitude can't solely be about my not coming to get you first." She swallowed hard, realizing the significance of what she was saying.

Last night…

Last night had been one of the most beautiful nights of her life. She'd made love to a man who in equal parts maddened and delighted her. She'd felt emotions she'd never experienced before. And she'd lain in his arms, thinking that they'd turned a corner of sorts and were moving into uncharted territory. Not just for her but for him, as well. And she'd openly welcomed the prospect.

But as she stood looking at him now, she realized that he must have backtracked emotionally when she wasn't paying attention. Essentially he had moved to a place where he could safely reerect his barriers against her.

He looked away. "I'm going to go restart the generator. I'm sure there are worried people out there who would like to know our guests are okay."

What he wasn't saying was that he could also

probably get an idea of when they might all be rescued. Surely by now the storm was close to blowing itself out or moving on, even if it seemed to be raging harder than before.

Natalie had been born and raised in Courage Bay and knew these severe storms well. One minute they could be hell on earth, the next the wind would stop and the sun's yellow rays would break through the clouds and all would be okay again.

She wrapped her arms around herself, watching as Dan went back outside. She wondered if the simple reemergence of the sun would be enough to make things between them okay again.

The door closed soundly behind him and she gave a little start.

Last night she'd opened a part of herself to him that had everything to do with trust. And she'd known he'd done the same with her. So what had happened between then and now? What had motivated him to shut her out?

It wasn't easy, this falling in love stuff. She'd fought her attraction to him as adamantly as he'd fought his for her. But ultimately neither of them could deny what was happening between them.

Correction. She couldn't.

Dan, on the other hand, appeared more than capable of going back to the way things were before they'd made love.

The knowledge both shocked and hurt her.

"Natalie?"

She looked down at Trilby, who was tugging on the hem of her shirt.

Despite the unbearable pain swirling around inside her, and the tears burning her eyes, Natalie crouched down to face the girl. "What is it, Trilby?"

"Is everything going to be all right?"

"Everything's going to be fine, honey. Everything's going to be just fine." Natalie nodded, but in her heart she feared that nothing would be all right ever again.

DAN MANAGED TO GET WORD out on the Moorhead family's safety, and also succeeded in getting through to coast guard headquarters, where staff patched through a line to the fire station.

He glanced at the little girl standing nearby, raptly watching him as he waited to speak with his daughter.

It seemed that the instant Debra had received word that Dan was stranded, she'd bunked at the firehouse, waiting for more news.

"Daddy?"

His daughter's voice came over the radio, her relief evident despite the thick static.

"Hi, baby," Dan murmured, briefly closing his eyes. Her voice sounded different in light of all that had happened over the past three days. Or maybe her voice wasn't different but rather he had changed in some irrevocable way he had yet to figure out.

"What happened?" his daughter was saying. "Are you all right? Are you hurt?"

Dan listened to her rapid-fire questions and grinned. "I'm fine, Deb. Just fine." Or at least he would be once he got back to his familiar life on the mainland.

"And Natalie?" Debra asked.

He glanced at the woman in question, standing on the other side of the console, her arms wrapped around herself. "She's fine, too. Look, Deb, I've got to end the transmission. I promise I'll be home before you know it, okay?"

There was a brief silence, then she said, "Okay. I love you, Dad."

"Me, too, honey," Dan said quietly.

He switched off the mike, then the radio.

"The generator is running on fumes now," he said. "So I'll just let it run itself out."

Natalie had moved to the sink and was washing the mugs, her profile somber.

"I have some fuel in the boat," Ken said, trying to get up. "A good ten gallons. Will that do?"

His wife clamped a hand on his shoulder and Dan grinned at him. "That will do just fine."

He headed for the door, grabbing his windbreaker on the way out. He went to close the door, but Natalie was right behind him.

"What are you doing?" he asked, his tone sharper than he'd intended.

She blanched. "I'm going with you."

"I don't need you."

His words fell between them like shards of broken crystal. Dan prepared to clarify himself, to say that he meant he didn't need her help with the fuel. But when she began backing away from him, a suspicious brightness in her eyes, he gritted his teeth and turned around.

He hated when women cried.

More than that, he hated himself for making Natalie cry.

CHAPTER THIRTEEN

NATALIE HAD NEVER BEEN so upset. She paced the station floor, back and forth, forth and back, until she was sure she was making not only herself dizzy, but also little Trilby, who watched from the cot across the room.

Finally Natalie grabbed her rain slicker. "I'm going to go out and help him." *Whether he wants my help or not,* she silently added.

When she stepped onto the porch, Spike came out after her. At least one familiar male wanted her company. She reached down and patted him. "Stay close, buddy."

He wagged his tail and followed her down the slippery stairs.

Natalie fought to keep upright in the fierce wind, anger fueling her steps. For the past hour she had been unable to confront Dan in the way he needed to be confronted. But she fully intended to remedy that now. Their relationship seemed to swing from one extreme to the next, and that had to stop.

Relationship? Did they even have a relationship?

She lifted her chin into the wind. Yes, they did. They'd been as intimate as a man and a woman could be. They'd bared far more than just their bodies to each other, and she wasn't going to allow Dan to pretend they hadn't.

So he had issues. So did she. She hadn't gone to the fire station the other day thinking she wanted to get involved with him. In fact, it had been the exact opposite. She'd gone to close her case file on him, effectively tucking him away into the past.

She remembered his angry, puckered burn wound and flinched. Dan needed medical attention and that would place him in her professional life for a good portion of the foreseeable future.

Of course, that was if he'd listened to what she'd told him.

She clenched her teeth tightly together. There were too many ifs when it came to Dan's personal life. His professional life was another story. When confronted with a blaze, he didn't stand outside wondering if he should wait for it to blow itself out because that would be easier. Instinct propelled him to send in his team, hoses spraying, ready to do battle with the fiery dragon.

Then why did he do the opposite in life? Why was he behaving as if it was best to wait for whatever was happening between them to blow itself out rather than grab on to every moment and live it to its fullest?

She didn't know, but she sure as hell intended to find out.

The wet sand impeded her progress and she stumbled over a piece of driftwood, making her realize she wasn't paying attention to where she was going.

Spike, who'd been trotting along by her side, suddenly stopped.

Natalie hesitated, watching his old body stiffen in alert, his nose pointed, his tail still and rigid.

"What is it, boy?" she asked.

He gave a shrill bark, which was instantly muffled by the harsh wind, and fixed his gaze on something in front of them.

Natalie squinted through the rain, her anger turning into fear as she spotted Dan some fifty feet away…being held at gunpoint.

HE'D BEEN CAUGHT *with his guard down…*

Dan stared at the man who he suspected had inhabited the island along with him and Natalie since the first day. A man who had managed to keep from crossing paths with them up until now. A man who had come out of hiding to get the same fuel Dan had come for.

"That's far enough!" the man called. "Back away from the boat!"

Dan had no doubt this was the prowler K-9 Officer Cole Winslow had been tracking on Courage Bay

Mountain the day of the mudslide. All the physical characteristics matched up. Five foot eleven. Dark curly hair and blue eyes. A teardrop tattoo under his left eye that indicated a gang killing, one that more than likely had taken place a decade earlier, in his youth.

For the most part, Courage Bay was a serene city. A place where you could raise your children without the fears that larger metropolises faced. But recently even Courage Bay had seen an increase in the types of criminal activity that plagued larger urban centers. Dan had only to think of the warehouse explosion that had nearly taken his life and left him scarred three months ago.

But not even he would have guessed he'd be squaring off with a fugitive while stranded on S-hamala Island in the middle of a severe storm.

"I said get away from the boat!" the man shouted over the roar of the wind, wielding a .45 revolver in front of him.

Dan held up his hands and stepped back a couple of feet, eyeing the firearm. It wasn't your run-of-the-mill weapon, especially not one favored by gun-toting criminals. More than likely it was a collector's item the guy had stolen from one of the houses on Courage Bay Mountain. "Hey, whatever you say," Dan called out.

A few curses filled the air between them. "I guess even small-time minds like yours are capable of putting two and two together," the prowler said.

"I've known about you since the moment I got off that chopper," Dan bluffed.

Although he'd suspected that he and Natalie weren't alone on the island, he'd had no idea their fellow cast-away was the prowler Cole had been looking for.

"The question is, now that we've come face-to-face, what do we do?"

Dan shrugged, his hands still up in the air as he discreetly scanned the landscape for anything he could use to protect himself, to tip the scales of power in his favor. "Easy. I let you take the fuel, and you let me return to the cabin. And things go back to the way they were before."

His adversary's eyebrows shot up. "You'll *let* me take the fuel?" He considered the firearm in his hand. "I don't think you're in a position to let me do anything, Egan."

The guy knew his name....

"That's right, I know who you are. I read the paper. You're that guy, that fire chief, who almost died in that warehouse explosion three months ago."

Dan narrowed his eyes. "What do you know about that?"

"Do you mean did I have a hand in it? No. Not my style."

"That's right. Breaking into people's homes and making off with things they worked hard for is more your style, isn't it?"

"The people we're talking about don't have a clue what's important in life."

"And you do?"

Dan knew he shouldn't be challenging the fugitive. His criminal past might not be violent, but that could change depending on the circumstances.

"Those people think nothing of blowing money on fancy vases and pricey paintings. They don't care if there are needy people out there."

"Like you."

The prowler grinned. "Yes. Exactly like me."

"So you see yourself as a Robin Hood of sorts. Only the poor in question is yourself."

"Mmm. I like the sound of that. Robin Hood."

The wind was picking up, blowing against Dan's back, and the rain pelting his face made him blink. "And is it worth the risk?"

The prowler stood a little ways back, slightly protected from the elements by the thick stand of pines. "Risk? What risk are you talking about?"

"Of capture."

"By you?"

Dan squinted at his opponent. "By anyone. I may be willing to look the other way because, hey, you've never done anything to me. But the next guy you come across might not be so forgiving."

Out of the corner of his eye, Dan caught movement. At first he thought it was bits of tree branches being blown around by the storm. But then he saw Spike leap at the prowler's right arm, which held the gun, and a loud alarm went off in his head.

If Spike was out, so was Natalie….

ONE MINUTE NATALIE had been considering the many ways she could give Dan what-for for his unacceptable behavior, the next she was watching helplessly as Spike pounced on a man she'd never laid eyes on before. A man who was holding a gun on Dan.

"No!" she heard Dan shout as he lunged for the stranger.

A shot rang out and Natalie's feet faltered on the sand. Then she was running flat out. She watched as Dan and the other man fell to the ground like two solid redwoods cut at the base, Spike landing on the beach next to them.

Who'd been shot? Where was the gun? She wildly tried to get a handle on the situation as she reached the site. A red stain was growing quickly on Spike's hindquarters. But Natalie suppressed the need to attend to him, too afraid the same might happen to Dan.

She slammed her foot against the gunman's right hand, pinning it on the ground just as he kicked Dan off him. Quickly she grabbed the firearm and launched it toward the churning waves as Dan fell heavily against the sailboat, then slumped to the sand.

"Dan!" Natalie rushed toward him, her heart beating loudly in her ears as she watched his eyelids droop, as if he was a hairbreadth away from unconsciousness.

"Don't let him leave…."

Natalie leaned to prop him up, trying to check the back of his head for contusions. "What?"

The storm blew around them, pelting them with stinging rain.

"Don't…let…him…get away."

Natalie looked over her shoulder at the place where the man had been. Too late. He was gone.

SOMETIME LATER, Natalie stood at the window of the cabin, watching as Dan carried Spike's lifeless body, wrapped in a blanket, through the heavily pouring rain. She hugged herself tightly, tears burning her eyes at the sight of the man and his lost best friend.

It was her fault. She knew it. She should never have gone out when Dan had requested she stay behind. And she shouldn't have taken Spike with her.

But blame and guilt wouldn't change the fact that Spike had died saving his master's life. And that his master was braving the elements to put him in the shed until he could give the fallen hero a proper burial.

Dan hadn't had anything to say to her. He had refused Jeremy's offer of help, so she'd stayed off to one side of the room, a spectator instead of a participant.

Hadn't she already done enough?

She stood staring out into the storm, her brain

numb, her heart aching for the strong man and his beloved dog.

A half hour later he reentered the cabin, soaked to the skin, his face drawn into somber lines. Natalie couldn't bring herself to look into his eyes for fear of what she might find there. She stayed where she was and turned back toward the window, listening as he explained to Ken and Nessa about the fugitive that shared the island with them. While Natalie had tossed the gun into the bay, there was no guarantee he didn't have another firearm or flare gun or something he could use to harm or threaten them.

"So we're all going to have to be vigilant," Dan said. "Now that he knows we know he's here, there's no telling what he's capable of. He's kept clear of the cabin until now, but...well, he might decide he's tired of braving the elements by himself and try to gain access."

"You mean hold us hostage?" Natalie asked.

Dan finally met her gaze, and she read the intensity in his eyes. "It's a possibility, yes." Though he'd sent the children to the other side of the cabin to play cards, their stillness indicated they'd heard every word he'd said. "Since you're already at the window, why don't you take first watch?" he suggested to Natalie.

She shivered and nodded, then turned her attention back toward the rain-washed window. Out of the corner of her eye she could see Dan slant the back of a chair under the doorknob, then lay a thick piece of wood on the seat, presumably for use as a weapon.

"You should change out of those wet things," Natalie said, then immediately wished she'd remained silent.

He didn't reply. But she felt a moment's relief when he took his dry clothes and disappeared into the bathroom, coming out a moment later, having changed. He crossed to the communications radio and switched it on, apparently having added the gasoline they'd salvaged from the wreck to the generator's fuel tank. She listened as he outlined the situation to the mainland coast guard harbor patrol. They would alert the authorities and try to get a craft out as soon as weather permitted.

Dan signed off but remained seated at the radio, looking as drained as Natalie felt. She straightened her spine and turned back toward the window. After the chopper had hit the sand, Natalie had had no doubt that she and Dan would survive their time on the island. But after what had happened with Spike... well, all that had changed.

Everything had changed.

HE SHOULD THANK HER.

Dan sat at the radio, staring at the knobs and switches without really seeing them. The silence in the room was palpable. The grief he felt over Spike's death was a deep, gnawing ache inside him.

But if Natalie hadn't come out and brought Spike with her, who was to say what would have happened to Dan himself? He glanced over his shoulder at her, standing at the window, her posture stiff.

"Mr. Dan?"

He turned toward the little girl to his left. She stood clutching a blanket to her chest, her blue eyes big and bright. She reminded him so much of Debra when she was young that he had to blink to make sure it wasn't her.

"Is Spike gone?"

Her parents had kept the girl away from the scene when he and Natalie had taken the dog up to the shed. The bullet that had entered Spike's chest and exited his hindquarters had instantly taken his life. A shot that might have been meant for Dan.

Dan nodded slowly. "Yes, sweetie, I'm afraid he is."

"Because that bad man shot him?"

He nodded again, his need to reassure Trilby stronger than his need to grieve his own loss. "Spike was doing his job."

"His job?"

Dan nodded, then scooted back so he could hoist the four-year-old into his lap. "Uh-huh. You see, Spike used to be a fire dog. You know what that is, don't you? No? He used to go out on fire runs with me and the other firemen. He'd go into burning houses to see if there were any little girls or boys inside that needed to be rescued."

"But he wasn't a fire dog anymore?"

He shook his head. "No, he wasn't. He had to retire a couple years ago, and he came home to live with me."

"Retire?"

"Yes. That means he got too old to be rushing into burning houses."

Not unlike himself.

"Poor Spike."

Dan smiled softly, remembering how put out the dalmatian had been when he'd been left at home all day. Dan had taken the dog to visit the station every now and again, but whenever he did, Spike had to be restrained from jumping onto the back of a truck when they went out on a run, despite his age and arthritis.

It had been a long time since he'd thought of Spike as a member of the firefighting team.

It had been a long time since he'd remembered much of anything apart from Ellie's death. A long time since he'd remembered the way he himself had been, before age had curtailed some of his own activities.

But there was a difference between merely aging and being old. He was coming to understand that now. He was forty-five, not ninety. And, yes, what was happening between him and Natalie scared him more than a four-alarm blaze, but using his age as an excuse not to become involved with her was nothing if not stupid.

For some reason he couldn't comprehend, he felt enormously grateful for the little girl and her innocent questions. Not only had she chased away a bit of the heartache connected to Spike's death, she'd given Dan an unexpected shove away from the grief that had gripped him so intensely ever since he'd lost Ellie. Trilby had shed light on the self-pity he'd felt since being promoted to fire chief.

And revealed him for the old…no, the aging fool that he was.

He glanced at Natalie's stiff back. Maybe he should be old enough to know better, but damn, he'd live to regret it if he didn't give Natalie and him a chance.

Dan rested his forehead briefly against Trilby's and smiled. "Yes, poor Spike."

He toyed with the radio, bringing it back on line. A conversation with Godfrey right now would help both him and the little girl focus on something outside themselves.

And hopefully help him find a way to apologize to the lady doc.

CHAPTER FOURTEEN

NATALIE COULDN'T BE positive, but it appeared the storm was beginning to subside. The wind didn't seem nearly as fierce, the sea seemed to be calming down, and the steady rain was pounding directly down on the roof instead of hitting it in uneven waves.

She glanced at her watch to verify the time. Almost dark and it was only four in the afternoon. Behind her the Moorhead family slumbered, exhausted by their three-day ordeal on the storm-swept bay. Just looking at them—the two adults on two cots they'd tied together, as if they couldn't bear to be apart for even a nap; the little girl cuddled between them, while Jeremy slept on the floor at their heads— filled her heart with an unnamed something.

Longing. That's what she felt. She knew such a tremendous longing for a family of her own that it nearly took her breath away.

Dan came to stand next to her. "I thought you could use some of this."

She warily accepted the cup of coffee he offered, trying to interpret the motive behind his actions.

"Thanks." She tucked her hair behind her ear and took a long sip.

The silence that settled between them stretched her nerves to the breaking point.

"Look, Dan, I—"

"Natalie, I just wanted—"

Both started, then stopped talking at the same time.

Natalie blinked at him, wondering what he could have to say. She lifted her hand. "Let me go first. It may negate what you wanted to say."

He nodded, considering the contents of his coffee cup.

Natalie cleared her throat. "I wanted to tell you how sorry I am for coming out earlier when you asked me not to. If I had stayed behind, or had left Spike in the cabin—" Her voice caught and she looked everywhere but at Dan. In her mind was an image of him carrying Spike from the cabin, heading out into the storm, man and dog.

"Are you done?" he asked.

She swallowed back the emotion clogging her throat and slowly nodded, bracing herself for what he might say.

She was surprised by the feel of his fingers on her chin. He lifted her face to look at him, and she nearly gasped at the soft smile that curved his lips.

"If you hadn't come out earlier—with Spike—I might be the one lying in the shed right now, Natalie."

She narrowed her eyes at him, certain she was hearing things. "What did you just say?"

This couldn't be Dan Egan. The guy who went out of his way to keep her at an emotional distance. The guy who held on to a grudge with both hands because it was easier than trying to deal with it.

"That's right. I came over here to thank you for heading out when you did."

Natalie was filled with so many conflicting emotions that she felt dizzy with them.

"I'd suspected that we weren't alone on the island from the beginning. But I hadn't taken extra measures to protect you...to protect us. That was my fault. And running into the gunman was also my fault."

"You're not to blame for Spike's death," Natalie whispered.

Dan's blue, blue eyes held so much pain. "I'm not laying blame at anyone's feet for that, Nat."

For a brief moment, she wondered if they were talking about Spike at all. Wondered if in some small way Dan was referring to his wife's death.

Was that why he was having such a hard time moving beyond it? Did he somehow feel that he himself was to blame?

She was about to ask him when Jeremy got up to use the bathroom.

Natalie stared at her feet, unsure what to say. Or if she should say anything.

It seemed both she and Dan were blaming themselves for things that neither of them had any control over.

But recognizing that fact was one thing. How to stop the destructive habit and move on to more positive territory was something else entirely.

She glanced up at Dan. At his strong, handsome features. His all-too-kissable mouth. Then she kissed him.

THE LAST THING DAN HAD expected Natalie to do was kiss him. The move was so unanticipated he'd barely had time to return the gesture before she pulled back and smiled at him.

"What was that for?" he asked quietly, surprised by his complete physical reaction to the brief contact.

She shrugged, then took a sip of her coffee. "I don't know. I felt like kissing you so I did."

He squinted at her.

"Don't you ever do things because something moves you to?"

"No," he said. "Never."

"Me, neither." She looked at him long and hard. "But I've decided it's long past time I started to."

She turned back toward the window, staring out into the growing darkness. "I think the storm's finally letting up."

Dan continued looking at her for long moments, not really registering her words as he took in her pretty profile, her tangle of dark hair, her slim figure.

Then he glanced out the window, moving flush against her side as he did so.

She was right. The storm was beginning to abate.

Which meant it was only a matter of time before the coast guard could get them off the island.

The thought, and his gut reaction to it, caught him off balance. He almost wished the storm would continue.

He grimaced. That didn't make any sense, did it? In the beginning, he'd been nothing short of pissed off to be stuck here with the beautiful Dr. Natalie Giroux. Now…

Now he found himself wanting to spend more time with her. He wanted to kiss her again. Wanted to make love to her again. And for some inexplicable reason, he was afraid that when they returned to the mainland, the opportunity for him to do either would be taken firmly out of his hands.

No, the reason he was afraid he might not see her again wasn't really all that hard to figure out. The truth was, he hadn't been ready for Natalie. And he suspected he'd never be ready for the attraction he felt for her or the bond that was growing between them, no matter how hard he tried to combat it.

But back on the mainland...

Back on the mainland, their lives were so different there would be absolutely zero opportunity for their paths to cross.

You could always ask her on a date, a small voice said inside his head.

His jaw tightened. A date. Him, the fire chief, asking her, a doctor, out on a date after what had passed between them. The idea seemed ludicrous. Where would he take her? To the movies? To dinner? And what would they talk about? The storm? Spike's death? They shared nothing in common except what had happened to them during the past three days.

He glanced over his shoulder at the Moorhead family. Jeremy had since come out to rejoin them, and was lying under a blanket on the floor. If not for the Mooreheads and the fact that the prowler was lurking out there somewhere, capable of doing Lord knew what, Dan would have radioed the coast guard and lowered the urgency of their rescue. But he couldn't. Anyway, to even consider doing so was nothing short of stupid. He needed to be back on the mainland with his men. He needed to bury Spike.

He needed to look at his life in the new light Natalie had inadvertently shone on it, and figure out where he went from here.

"Someone's out there."

Dan was instantly alert. Had the prowler decided to make his move now? Was he out there strategizing, figuring out a way to get inside the house?

Dan moved to pick up the length of wood resting on the chair, but Natalie grasped his arm. He stared into the darkness. But it wasn't the prowler Natalie was looking at in the dark. It was a light—more specifically a spotlight—that her attention was drawn to.

The coast guard had come out sooner than expected.

NATALIE STOOD on the hard-packed sand of the beach, the rain stinging her exposed cheeks and forehead. Night had fallen and the only light came from the small coast guard cutter and the flashlight she held as Dan helped Jeremy climb into the orange raft that would take him, his mom and sister out to the cruiser. The dock the craft normally would have used had become unstable in the storm. She watched as the motor-propelled raft headed out across the inky, choppy water.

All too soon it would be coming back for her and Dan.

And all too soon they would be back home, returning to their individual and very separate lives.

The wind had picked up again while they were transporting Ken to the beach, and the storm they'd thought was winding down appeared to be gearing up for one last assault before it moved on. Fortunately, the injured man had made it safely out to the cutter. Natalie watched now as the normally stable raft tipped almost vertical on a high wave. She held her breath, afraid Jeremy, his mother and sister would be spilled out into the angry sea. In the dark it would be impossible to see them.

The wave crashed against the shore. Natalie craned her neck to check the status of the raft. Thankfully, it was stable once again, although it seemed to be chugging toward the cutter more slowly after having taken on water.

Dan rejoined her on the beach, a silent presence. But at least he wasn't avoiding her company anymore. She was aware of him beside her, tall and strong and capable.

The coast guard crew helped the remaining members of the family board the boat, which was anchored a good hundred yards away. Natalie shivered, readying herself for the trip back to reality.

She was startled when the cutter blew its horn and set off across the bay. Dan took the flashlight from her, giving the crew a brief wave.

She pushed away the hair the wind had blown into her eyes. "What…why are they leaving without us?"

"The storm's gearing back up for another hit. The captain was worried they might get stuck out here if they didn't make a run for the mainland now." Dan looked at her, his face devoid of emotion. "They'll come back for us in the morning, weather permitting."

Natalie's heart skipped a beat.

She and Dan would be alone together for one more night....

Awareness slid over her, making her skin tingle, igniting heat deep in her belly.

He put his arm over her shoulders. "Come on, let's go back inside. I don't know how safe it is out here."

For one brief, sweet moment Natalie had forgotten about the threat hiding somewhere in the shadows. On the island was a fugitive who had more than likely heard the boat and observed that Natalie and Dan had stayed behind.

She entered the cabin and Dan followed, bolting the door and propping the chair under the knob. Then he hoisted a bag of supplies he must have gotten from the coast guard crew onto the table and went through it. As she picked up blankets and straightened the cabin, she saw him take out a flare gun, lantern fuel and a couple of tightly sealed packages of what she could only hope was food.

Sure enough, Dan unwrapped the Meals Ready to Eat. She watched as he opened a couple of the larger packages, slid smaller ones inside them, then added water, explaining that they held flameless heating devices. He spread one of the gray wool blankets over the table and set the dinners out as if he were serving a five-star dinner for two, putting the glowing lantern in the middle of the table.

"Hungry?" he asked.

Not the most romantic invitation she'd ever had, but definitely the most welcome.

"Just give me a minute to wash up."

She gathered her purse and a clean dish towel, then disappeared into the bathroom, closing the door after her. She leaned against the smooth wood for a long moment, filling her lungs with a deep breath. There wasn't much she could do to improve her appearance, but she felt compelled to try. She was wearing the same clothes she'd pretty much been wearing for three days. She didn't have a hair dryer or her hair products to try to tame the beast that currently resided on top of her head, even if she had managed to wash it the night before under the faucet with a bar of soap.

She dared open her eyes to study the reflection staring back at her in the mirror.

Strangely, she discovered she didn't look all that bad. Unfamiliar, maybe, but not repulsive. She'd been using straightening formulas and a hair blower for so many years that she'd forgotten how curly her hair was. Even damp, it naturally framed her face, emphasizing her high cheekbones and forehead and making her eyes appear lighter. She tugged open the collar of her blouse, noticing a rosy tinge to her skin

from her cheeks to her chest, and even without lipstick, her lips had some color to them.

She unbuttoned her blouse and slid it off, along
with the borrowed cargo pants and her underwear,
wetting the towel under the faucet and soaping up.
She'd never given herself a full sponge bath before,
but considering the lack of a shower or tub, this would
have to work. She dragged the soft, soapy cloth over
her arms, then down her sides, stopping at her bare
thighs. Everywhere she touched she felt hy-
persensitive. Absently she rinsed the towel, then
soaped up again, continuing down her other side, then
stopping again just before reaching between her legs.

Natalie swallowed hard, unable to remember a
time when she'd been so aware of herself as a woman.

After rinsing the towel again, she slid the soapy
cloth over her abdomen, not stopping until the wet-
ness dripped between her legs.

She shivered.

A soft rap sounded on the door. "Natalie? Are
you okay?"

She felt as if she'd just gotten caught watching an
X-rated video.

"Fine—I'm fine," she said, her voice cracking on
the word *fine*.

A pause, then, "Dinner's getting cold."

She smiled and reached for a blanket she'd hung
on the back of the door earlier. After quickly dry-

ing herself, she put her clothes back on with the exception of her panties, which she washed out and left on the towel rack to dry, as she'd been doing every night.

But whereas she would normally be climbing into the cot to sleep by herself, tonight she would be sitting across from Dan at the table, sans undies, feeling more than a little naughty and hopeful.

After applying a bit of mascara and lip gloss, she opened the door to find Dan standing directly outside.

Her heart skipped a beat and her palms grew instantly damp.

He grinned at her. "There's no dress code for this particular restaurant, Doc."

She allowed him to pull out a chair for her, then waited for him to take the one across from her before considering the dinner fare.

"I thought you'd prefer the chicken," he said. "But if you'd rather have the beef…"

"Chicken's fine," she told him. The meal looked as good as anything the Courage Bay Bar and Grill had to offer.

There were no curtains on the windows, no way to hide themselves from prying eyes. She'd started to cover the windows with blankets, but Dan had pointed out that in order for the fugitive to get a peek inside, he'd have to climb up on the porch. And if he did so, they'd want to see him.

Would he do that? Would he be willing to put himself at risk?

She supposed it depended on whether or not he'd run out of food, and how desperate he was.

"Natalie, I…"

She gazed into Dan's eyes. He looked uneasy and his movements as he ate were awkward.

"Please, don't say anything, Dan. Whatever happens, let's just try to enjoy tonight, okay?"

His gaze raked her face, leaving her feeling exposed and vulnerable, as if she'd revealed more than she was comfortable doing.

He nodded curtly. "Okay."

Outside, the wind howled around the cabin as if determined to shake it from its posts. Natalie shivered and reached for the radio sitting on a corner of the table. She switched it on, relieved when the static-filled sound of big band music filled the room, battling with the roar of the wind.

She looked up to find Dan watching her, a grin playing around his mouth.

"What?" she asked.

He didn't respond for a long moment, then slowly put his fork down and shook his head. "Nothing. It's just that…I think you're the only woman I know who could be stranded in the middle of a storm and think to play music."

Natalie smiled as she toyed with her food. Even

though it had been three days since she'd had a good, solid meal, and her empty stomach seemed to constantly be gnawing at her, she suddenly had no appetite. "When you're in my line of work, you have to learn how to soothe your patients as well as yourself. Music has always done that for me."

He squinted slightly, bringing the crinkly lines on either side of his eyes into sharp relief.

Natalie found them attractive. She decided he must have had a baby face when he was younger, making him look a lot less than his age. He had the kind of face that a guy with his strength would have to grow into.

And he had grown into it wonderfully. She could look at him for hours without tiring.

"Do you ever get attached to your patients?" he asked quietly.

The question surprised her. "Are you asking about yourself and any attachment that might be forming?"

He grinned. "No. I'm talking in general."

"Good, because I would have had to lie if you were referring to yourself, and tell you I never get attached to my patients. That I always keep things strictly professional."

With a chuckle, he sat back, moving his coffee mug in circles on the table.

"Yes, I get attached to my patients. In med school, they tell you not to. But what I do is so much a part of who I am that I can't separate my work from life, you know?"

She saw understanding in his eyes and knew a moment of gratitude. So few people seemed to comprehend why she worried about Jessica Woodward, who had suffered third-degree hot grease burns on the front of her legs while she was cooking. Natalie even called her at home at night to see how she was doing and to make sure she applied her topical ointment. No one seemed to grasp why, when she was at the MetroHealth Medical Center in Cleveland as a long-term resident, she'd spent hours on end reading *Moby Dick* to a patient who'd suffered burns to more than ninety percent of his body in a house fire while trying to save his wife.

But somehow she sensed that Dan appreciated what she was saying. She also sensed he admired her for it.

"Takes a strong person to do what you do," he said quietly.

She forked up her buttered noodles. "No, it takes a strong person to do what *you* do every day. What I do…well, I think it takes heart."

Dan shook his head. "I've been thinking about this a lot over the past couple days, you know? Seeing as we haven't had much else to do."

His eyes shone in a way that suggested he was thinking about one of the things they had done to pass the time.

"Anyway, what I do may take physical strength, but what you do…it takes strength of character to go to work day in and day out, face what you do, and still do a good job."

Natalie felt a flush work its way up from her chest to her neck and cheeks. "I think that's the nicest compliment anyone's ever given me."

"I'm not trying to compliment you, Natalie. I'm stating facts."

She searched his handsome face, so thankful for him in that moment that her chest hurt. "And what happens to us after this, Dan?"

CHAPTER FIFTEEN

A SIMPLE THANK-YOU WOULD have done.

Dan stared at Natalie, having momentarily forgotten that nothing was simple when it came to the lady doc. At least not with him and her.

"Have you thought about it at all?" she asked, apparently giving up any pretense of eating, and pushing her meal away so she could lean her forearms on the table. "What happens when we get back home?"

"All the time."

Dan was surprised the words had come out of his mouth. And so was Natalie, if her expression was anything to go by.

"And?"

He carefully considered her.

To answer her question would be to suggest that he'd come to some sort of conclusion. But the truth was he hadn't. The only certainty he knew was here and now. The mainland and home seemed so far away as to be on another planet. He couldn't possibly give her an answer that either one of them would be happy with.

"And…" he began, dragging the word out as he considered what to do. "I think you were right earlier when you asked me not to say anything. That we should just concentrate on enjoying tonight."

What went unsaid was that it might be their last night together.

He watched her swallow hard, then nod. "I did say that, didn't I?"

He smiled, and she smiled back. "Yes, you did."

"All right then, what do you propose we do?"

There was something refreshingly forthright and unspeakably sexy about her question. Because the answer to it lay right there in her expressive face. She wanted him as much as he wanted her. Right now—while the storm still raged and they were alone together, the world forgotten for a few more precious hours.

Dan pushed himself from his chair and went to stand in front of her, holding out his hands. She didn't hesitate to grasp them, and he gently pulled her up. Their bodies weren't touching, yet he felt as if she was touching him everywhere.

So beautiful. So genuine. When he bent his head to hers, he knew on a subconscious level that she would respond in just the way he wanted her to. And he wasn't disappointed. He slid his lips against hers, reveling in her softness, the sweetness of her kiss. She lifted her arms and linked her hands around the back of his neck, not forcing the kiss but rather coaxing it out of him. He felt for the buttons on her blouse, amazed at how easily he undid them, as if he'd been doing so all his life. He tugged the material open, then drew back slightly to take her in. Her breathing was ragged from their kisses and, he supposed, from his focused attention. Her slender midriff moved in and out, trembling, bringing into sharp relief the smooth slope of her breasts above the lacy cups of her bra.

He'd always been fascinated by women. Their smell, their softness, the mystifying way their minds worked. But this particular woman… In the beginning, his attraction to Natalie Giroux had baffled and angered him, but now that he'd finally given in to it, given himself over to her, she completely and utterly captivated him.

Dan traced the upper ridge of her bra, watching as her breathing stopped briefly, then started again, raggedly. He'd done that. Affected her in such a profound way. He rested his fingertips over where he guessed her heart to be, finding the all-important organ pounding as hard as his was. He looked deep into her eyes, deciding he would never look at chocolate in quite the same way again.

"Touch me…please."

Natalie's soft plea almost made Dan groan. He opened his hand to cup her soft breast through the lacy material, feeling the hard peak, which seemed to speak as loudly as her words.

She lowered her arms from his neck and reached behind her. Within moments the lace was held in place only by his stroking fingers. He lifted his hand and watched as the scrap of fabric dropped forward, as far as the straps would allow.

This time Dan did groan. The tips of her breasts were rosy-red and puckered. He reached for the catch on her cargo pants as she shrugged the rest of the way out of her shirt and bra.

She isn't wearing any underwear....

The thought caught and held as he took in the crisp triangle of hair at the apex of her thighs. His gaze rose to hers and she smiled, as if liking him knowing that she had been as much aware of what was going to happen tonight as he had.

Dan pushed their uneaten dinner rations out of the way, then gently gripped Natalie's hips and lifted her to the blanket-covered table. He marveled at the way she stretched back, her skin glowing in the pale light from the lantern. He slid his hand up her bare thigh to her bottom, watching as her eyelids fluttered shut, her thick lashes a shadowy fringe against her flushed cheeks. Then she opened to him, and whatever plans he'd had to take things slow tonight were sorely challenged.

NATALIE HAD NEVER BARED herself so blatantly to another person before. But she did so now without reservation, without hesitation, and with full knowledge that the future yawned, an unknown quantity, before her.

Somewhere during the past few days she'd learned that control wasn't all it was cracked up to be; it was little more than an illusion. She didn't have any more control over her thoughts and emotions than the moon had over the sun. She'd slowly learned that sometimes it was enough to go with gut instinct. To follow her heart and watch as it led her to places she would never have otherwise gone.

And this man had unwittingly helped her realize that.

No longer did she feel Charles's absence from her life like a black void threatening to suffocate her. No longer did she feel the stifling guilt.

She watched Dan's hands as he slowly dragged them over her body, giving a little shiver at the sight of his darker skin against hers. A glint of light reflected off his wedding band. It was so much a part of him that she gave it no more notice than she did the soft jazzy song on the radio.

He drew his fingers down the middle of her stomach to her hips, allowing one thumb to burrow into the soft folds and press gently on the bit of flesh hiding there.

Natalie shivered again, wanting Dan with every part of her being.

Spreading her thighs, she hooked her legs around him and pulled him closer. It seemed surprising that he should still be completely dressed while she lay bare before him, so she nudged him back once more and stood up.

"Where are you—"

His words were cut off as she tugged his T-shirt from the waist of his jeans and pulled it up and over his head, being careful of his angry wound. Then she reached for the button to his jeans. Only when he finally stood before her naked, in all his glory, did Natalie stop to appreciate him. From the striking planes of his face to the rippled muscles of his abdomen, Dan was what could be called a man's man. An alpha male who knew no fear when it came to protecting others. Whose quick actions and even quicker intellect had saved many over the years.

And whose heart Natalie wanted to claim so badly she ached.

She turned him around until he was leaning against the table.

"What are you—"

"Shh." She pressed a finger against his lips. "Sit on top."

"Natalie…"

She smiled at him. "Don't think, Dan. Just do. Just…feel."

He did as she requested, sending another shiver quaking through her. He trusted her, and that touched her to the core.

Apparently impatient, Dan grasped her wrists, and within the blink of an eye, she was the one sitting on the table and he was cradled between her thighs, his need thick and pulsing against her damp flesh.

Natalie's eyelids fluttered closed as he slowly entered her, stretching her slick muscles to his girth, then slid in to the hilt.

Her response was immediate and explosive, and she felt herself shudder with the impact of her climax. His hands gripped her back, holding her tight, as if he were trying to ward off his own crisis. Natalie moaned, unable to catch her breath as her blood burned through her veins.

Long moments later she was still clinging to Dan's chest. He hadn't moved since he'd entered her, but now thrust forward with his powerful body, slowly and surely.

Natalie's tremors deepened. Every cell of her being seemed to vibrate with pleasure in response to the man holding her close. This man who filled her to overflowing not just physically, but emotionally.

Slowly he withdrew from her and gathered her into his arms. Natalie clutched him as he moved to the corner of the room where the blankets were piled. He gently laid her down, much as he had the first time they'd made love, then joined her.

She rolled to her side, forcing him to face her. Then she slid her leg over his, putting her sex in direct contact with his. He groaned as she led him to her welcoming flesh, then tilted her hips so that he was once again filling her.

Natalie's heart beat an intense rhythm as she watched the myriad emotions flick over Dan's face while they made love. Merely gazing at him set off a wildfire deep in her belly, and she felt precariously near the edge of orgasm and tears. He grasped her hips so he could fill her even deeper, and she threw her head back, clutching his shoulders as she rode wave upon wave of sensation.

And somewhere on the edges of her consciousness, she wondered how she was going to live without him now that she had finally found him.

DAN RAN HIS HAND over Natalie's silken skin under the blanket. She was sleeping soundly, her deep, even breathing soothing his soul.

He should be sleeping, too, but something had jarred him awake, and he lay in the dark, listening to the sounds around him.

Every now and again the windows rattled from a sudden gust of wind, but it was no longer a relentless assault. The storm was finally winding down for good, which meant the coast guard would be coming back for him and Natalie in a couple of hours.

A glance at the glowing numbers of his watch told him it was just before dawn. That surprised him. He thought he'd drifted off for a few minutes, but instead he'd slept for a few hours.

He looked down at the woman curved against his chest, her dark hair a riot of soft curls against his skin. She was as beautiful asleep as she was awake.

The scent of something intrusive set off an alarm in the back of his mind. It wasn't the smell of the generic soap he and Natalie had been using for the past couple days. Rather it was...

Gasoline.

In one easy motion he got up from the makeshift bed and grabbed his jeans and shoes. He drew in another deep breath and found the smell growing stronger.

"What...what is it?" Natalie asked when he stripped the blanket from her gloriously nude body and hauled her to a standing position.

"Get up and get dressed. We've got to get out of here. *Now.*"

An ominous *whoosh* sounded throughout the cabin. Dan grabbed a blanket and threw it over Natalie, then scooped her into his arms and rushed toward the exit. Kicking the chair from under the knob, he pulled the door open, only to find orange-and-yellow flames shooting in front of them, blocking the way.

Dan stepped back instantly, swinging Natalie to the side, out of harm's way, and setting her down. His heart was thudding in his chest, and in his mind's eye, he saw the fire he'd been trapped in three months ago. The scar on his side seemed to pulse and pull as he stared at the blaze in front of them.

He and Natalie and Spike had been the only ones to see the fugitive up close and personal. They were the only ones who would be able to identify him in a lineup.

Spike had paid for the privilege with his life.

Dan had the sickening feeling their friend planned the same fate for him and Natalie.

He looked down to see tiny tendrils of flame dancing between the cracks in the floorboards.

Something nudged against his arm, and he realized Natalie was standing beside him, dressed and holding a blanket she must have wet in the bathroom sink. He blinked at her. How long had he been standing there, staring at the flames? He began to cough as he took the blanket and started battling the flames eating up the porch.

Smoke billowed inside the small cabin, limiting sight and making breathing a challenge. Natalie disappeared, then came back moments later with another dripping blanket, helping to fight the flames.

"We need to get out of here!" he shouted to her,

and she nodded, soot smearing her right cheek, her eyes wide and overly bright.

He took his pocketknife out of his pants pocket, flicked open the blade, then pulled a chair beneath the hole in the ceiling and climbed up. Grabbing the edge of the tarp for leverage, he quickly sawed a long slit in the heavy fabric, the pain in his back and arm burning as if the fire were on top of him.

Once he'd finished, he stepped down from the chair and grasped Natalie's slender hips, pausing a moment to look into her wide eyes. In them he saw hope and fear and a trust that made it difficult to breathe in a way that had nothing to do with the smoke.

"Ready?"

She nodded again, and he hoisted her up through the hole, not releasing her until she had scrambled onto the roof. Using both the branch and beams to brace himself, Dan followed.

A SHORT TIME LATER Natalie stood on the beach coughing. All attempts to pull fresh air into her lungs seemed to force the smoke she'd inhaled deeper, until she feared she'd never breathe easily again. Distantly she realized the rain had stopped, and that the purple smear at the horizon indicated dawn was coming. The storm had finally moved on.

She blinked, staring at the cabin, which at that moment resembled the burning sun.

Dan stood next to her, coughing and holding his shoulder.

"Are you hurt?" she asked, stepping closer and trying to get a look at his bare back in the flickering light.

He stepped away from her. "It's not safe, Natalie. We have to move farther down the beach. Find shelter until the coast guard cutter arrives."

Natalie tried to make sense of his words, but she couldn't stop shivering as the damp dawn air seeped into her bones. An ominous creaking sound pulled her attention back to the burning cabin, and she watched as one of the front pilings holding the porch collapsed.

"Why hasn't he confronted us yet?" she heard Dan mutter, his jaw tight. In his fist he clutched the flare gun he'd brought out with him.

There! There was the sound again, Natalie realized. A man's voice. More specifically, the sound of a man calling for help.

Dan seemed to hear it, too.

Somewhere within the conflagration, the man who had tried to kill them must be trapped.

Cursing under his breath, Dan immediately started toward the burning structure.

Natalie desperately grabbed his arm. "What are you doing?"

The determination in his eyes made her shiver even more. "I can't just stand by and let him die, Nat."

The word *why* froze on the tip of her tongue. Of course Dan would have to save him. It didn't matter that the man was a thief. That he'd held Dan at gunpoint and shot Spike and set the cabin on fire while they were inside. Someone was in danger, and that's all that mattered to this courageous person who had made a career out of putting others' lives ahead of his own.

She swallowed hard, a revelation of sorts skittering along the edges of her mind. But she couldn't try to examine it now. She was too busy figuring out how she was going to save Dan if he got hurt trying to help the fugitive.

DAN POUNDED UPHILL to the right of the stairs in an attempt to gain access to the storage area. That must have been where their unwanted visitor had started the blaze. And where the flames that had been meant to harm Dan and Natalie had instead trapped him.

Blazing debris fell from overhead and Dan ducked to avoid being beamed by a chunk of falling flooring. He tried to make out something other than licking flames under the structure. He spotted the generator, where the amateur arsonist had likely siphoned off the fuel to set the fire, and climbed up closer to see if there was any sign of the guy.

The temperature was significantly hotter here at the fire's origin, and smoke billowed out, making Dan blink rapidly to clear his vision.

Where was the guy?

He felt the blow to the back of his head before he saw the man holding the board. Dan dropped to his knees, his eyesight blurring as the world tilted under him.

Another blow and he was lying facedown on the earth, flames surrounding him.

Their assailant hadn't needed help, after all. He'd merely moved on to plan B when he realized Dan and Natalie had escaped the cabin unharmed.

"I knew you'd have to play hero, Chief Egan," the fugitive said, still holding the board. "I'm flattered you wanted to save me. But it's too bad for you and your lady friend."

Dan's stomach tightened. With him out of the way, there wouldn't be anything between this sorry excuse for a man and Natalie.

"The coast guard will be here any minute," he rasped.

"Yes, they will. And they'll find both you and the lady burned to death in an awful accident. Kind of ironic, isn't it? The fire chief dying in a fire."

Dan couldn't let the monster he'd spent so much of his life fighting be credited for his death.

Another ominous creak sounded. His assailant stepped back, looking at the crackling structure above them. "Time for me to go pay a little visit to your lady love."

Dan kicked out his leg, catching the man at the ankles. A loud thump and his assailant was lying on the hard ground next to him, the board he held thudding against the generator. Dan scrambled to all fours, grabbed the board and shoved it against the man's neck.

"I should leave you here to burn," he growled, putting pressure on the board and causing the man to choke.

He watched as the fugitive, the man who had taken Spike's life and tried to take his and Natalie's, struggled to free himself, his face turning from mottled red to white as he fought for air. Dan knew he'd soon lose consciousness. That all he'd have to do was wait a few more moments and he'd have his revenge against this brute responsible for so much pain.

Instead, at the last moment he threw the board aside. Grabbing him by the collar, Dan dragged him away from the burning coast guard station.

NATALIE HAD NEVER FELT more relieved than when she saw Dan emerge from the wall of flames. He released the barely conscious man who had set fire to the cabin, then stumbled a few steps away. She rushed toward him, but when she reached out to embrace him, he dropped to his knees in front of her. Filled with alarm, she knelt on the ground and cupped his soot-covered face in her hands.

"Are you all right? Oh, God, please tell me you're okay."

He didn't seem to register her presence, though he was looking straight at her. Then he reached up to touch the side of her face, pressing his fingertips softly against her cheek.

"Have I ever told you how damn beautiful you are?" he said thickly, his voice hoarse from the smoke he'd inhaled.

A wave of emotion surged up from deep within Natalie as she searched his face. No, he hadn't. But it was something she could get used to hearing.

Unfortunately, she had the sinking feeling she'd never hear it again from Fire Chief Dan Egan.

As if underscoring her fear, across the bay came a blast from the coast guard cutter's horn.

CHAPTER SIXTEEN

"CHIEF, I WAS WONDERING if you'd had a chance to go over those rotation schedules."

Dan pushed his chair back from his desk. For a moment he hadn't seen the walls or the filing cabinet in his office at the fire station. His mind had been filled with an image of Dr. Natalie Giroux's face, her large mocha eyes, her plump mouth, her teasing smile.

For a moment there, he hadn't been back on the mainland at all, but still out on S-hamala Island, the lady doc nearby, everything that had happened pulling them closer together.

He'd been back from the island for two days. The storm had passed, and life as he knew it had pretty much gone back to normal.

Why was it, then, that nothing felt normal?

"What's that?" he asked, clearing his throat and rifling through the papers covering his desk.

Captain Joe Ripani leaned against the door frame, looking at him speculatively. "Hey, Dan.

Are you sure you're ready to come back to work? It looks like you could use a couple days off to recuperate."

"I had four damn days off where I did nothing but recuperate on that damn island," he muttered, finding the rotation schedules in the organized mess that was his desk and putting them on top of a pile.

Joe held his hands up in surrender. "Fine. Just making a suggestion." He gestured over his shoulder with his thumb. "I'll be in the rec room when you're ready to go over this stuff."

"Fine."

Ripani lingered for a moment, then finally left, shutting the door behind him.

Dan dropped his head into his hands.

Despite all that had happened on the island, he'd believed that once he returned to the normal, day-to-day grind, settled back into his routine, surrounded himself with all that was familiar, he'd find his way back to himself. To the man he was before Natalie had bared him of more than his clothes.

But nothing was familiar anymore. Nothing felt the same. Sure, everything looked just as it always had. His house was still stuffed with twenty years' worth of memories of Ellie. He'd gotten up the past two mornings, made his coffee, eaten the rolls Debra had brought by, and gone to work at the station, which thankfully remained unchanged.

Of course, one glaring difference was that Spike was no longer with him.

Dan stared at the picture of the dog he'd spent so much time with over the past twelve years. The afternoon after they'd returned from the island, he'd buried the old firehouse dog and fallen hero alongside Spot, his grandfather. A simple wood cross marked the site.

Meanwhile, the fugitive responsible for Spike's death and so much more was locked away in the county jail awaiting his bail hearing. Identified as Claude Decker by the authorities, he was not going to have an easy time of it. Especially since the rescue crew had found a dead body in one of the houses they'd dug out of the mudslide—a house Decker had burglarized. The dead man was producer Dylan Deeb.

Had Decker killed Deeb? Dan didn't know. What he did know was that Decker had tried to kill him and Natalie on the island. The rest…well, it was out of his hands now.

He stared at his desk, cluttered with schedules and reports and budget graphs. What he could usually see to with his eyes closed, now challenged him.

Dan almost felt as if someone had made off with the guy he used to be. He didn't recognize the man he saw in the mirror anymore. He lay in the bed he'd shared with Ellie and thought about another woman, wanting her, wishing she were there.

The phone on his desk rang. He snatched up the receiver and barked his name.

A moment later, he said, "No comment," then hung up.

Newspapers as far away as San Fran had been contacting him nonstop, looking for an angle on the island story and wanting to know what, if anything, he knew of Decker's connection to Deeb's murder. Every time Dan had walked outside the station his first day back, he'd been confronted by television cameras. He'd told the reporters that he'd already told them everything there was to know.

But that wasn't entirely true, was it? Because they didn't know that his life had changed radically during those four days on S-hamala Island. They couldn't know that one very beautiful lady doctor had essentially opened his eyes and showed him all he was missing, and had him so turned around he could no longer tell north from south.

They also couldn't know that he had neither seen nor talked to her since they'd climbed from that coast guard cutter, and that with every second that ticked by, the opportunity to do so was slipping away from him.

He heard the station phone ring over the intercom

and glanced at his watch. Damn. He was late for his lunch with Debra.

He opened the door and nearly ran into Joe Ripani.

"I'll get to those schedules when I come back," he grumbled, brushing by the squad captain.

TEN MINUTES LATER Dan was seated across from his daughter at the Courage Bay Bar and Grill, barely listening to what she was saying. He was suddenly filled with amazement that he had had anything to do with making the striking young woman across from him. How many times had he had lunch with Debra before Eleanor died? Once?

No, he realized, he'd never had lunch out with his daughter, just the two of them, before then. And only now did he realize what he'd been missing.

He grimaced at the realization. Last week he would have come to lunch, eaten his food, had an enjoyable conversation with his daughter, then gone back to work. He would not have marveled at the role he'd played in creating Debra. He wouldn't have felt regret or questioned whether he'd spent enough time with her before Ellie's death.

Before, he had just lived his life.

Now he was spending far too much time considering how he was living it. And one unforgettable woman deserved the credit for that.

Or was a more appropriate word *blame?*

"And then I pulled up my top and flashed everyone in the place."

Dan stared at his daughter's serious face as the last of her words registered. "What? What did you just say?"

Debra smiled wryly. "Just what I thought. You weren't listening to a single thing I said, were you?"

"Sure I was," he lied, lifting his coffee cup.

Her chagrin was obvious.

He leaned back in the booth, his burn wound feeling a little better now that he wasn't challenging it every five minutes. "Okay, maybe I wasn't listening to every word." He grinned at her. "But I was paying attention to the *way* you were saying them."

She blinked her wide blue eyes at him—eyes people told him looked exactly like his. But all he'd been able to see up till now were Ellie's eyes.

"Dad, are you okay?"

"Fine. I'm fine." He awkwardly cleared his throat. Physically, he might be all right. But he was coming to realize that other areas of his life needed some fine-tuning. "I was just thinking that how you were talking right now reminded me of when you were younger and used to chatter away at the dinner table. How you and I never had times like these together, just the two of us, before your mom died. About how you brought so much light and laughter to our lives when you were born."

Dan wasn't sure where all that had come from. He knew this new expressive streak had something to do with the changes he'd undergone while on that island, but exactly what, he couldn't say.

One thing he did know was that Debra appeared to be on the verge of tears.

"I said the wrong thing," he muttered, looking down at his coffee again.

And that was the problem with speaking out, wasn't it? The risk of saying something wrong.

Debra's small hand, so much like her mother's, pressed his. "No, Dad. What you said was exactly right."

He squinted at her. "Then why are you crying?"

She blinked rapidly as if unaware that her eyes were bright with unshed tears. "You know, that's not always a sign of sadness."

"So your tears, what you're feeling now, have to do with happiness?" he asked dubiously.

She nodded, then took her hand from his so she could blow her nose with her napkin.

"Women," he said under his breath. "Y'all are just too damn complicated."

That made her laugh—a happy sound he hadn't heard in a long time. "Men. You'll never figure out that it's all quite simple, actually."

Dan cracked a smile of his own. It seemed from the day Debra was born, she'd disagreed with him.

He'd say black, she'd say white. He'd say down, she'd say up. At one time it had seemed an endless source of annoyance for him.

He was surprised to find he now enjoyed it.

"Debra, I want to talk to you about your mom...."

Her cheeks paled, losing the color that had been there a moment ago. Dan looked at his sandwich, then glanced around the Courage Bay Bar and Grill, trying to find the words he needed. But he wasn't going to find them in the face of the owner, Larry Goodman. Or in the sliced beef on his plate. He glanced back at his daughter. The guidance he needed lay in her clear blue eyes.

"What is it?" she asked quietly, having given up all pretense of eating her Caesar salad.

"It's just...well, it's just that we never talk about her," he said. "That's not normal, is it? Someone who played such a large role in our lives, and we never talk about her?"

Debra's bottom lip briefly disappeared into her mouth as she shook her head. "Whenever I tried to say anything, you always tuned me out, or changed the subject until...until I stopped trying altogether."

Dan was surprised by what she was saying. Had he done that? Had he been the one who avoided talking about Ellie? "Really?"

She nodded. "Really."

He realized all at once that she was right, and

shifted uncomfortably in his seat. "Well, I'd like to talk about her now. And from now on."

Her smile touched him in places only his daughter could reach. "I'd like that. I'd like that a lot."

Silence fell between them, a silence that once might have left Dan squirming, looking at his watch, counting the minutes until he could leave and go back to the station.

But not now. Now he enjoyed the silence. It was…comfortable. And comforting.

Debra gave him a smile, then picked up her fork again. "Speaking of women…"

Dan squinted at her, his comfort level taking a sharp dip.

"What, exactly, happened between you and Natalie on that island?"

Carefully Dan picked up half of his sandwich and took a bite. "You don't know how good something is until you've had to go without for a stretch of time," he said with a full mouth.

He wasn't sure if he liked the angle of Debra's smile. "Are you talking about your sandwich…or Natalie?" she asked.

Dan started coughing so hard he nearly choked on the piece of beef halfway down his throat.

Immediately Debra got up and began patting his back, while the waitress brought him a fresh glass of water.

Long moments later, his breathing was back under control, Debra was reseated across from him and everyone in the restaurant had gone back about their business.

Except for his daughter.

Had he really thought he enjoyed the way she challenged him? Perhaps he'd come to the conclusion a little too quickly.

"I knew something had happened between the two of you on S-hamala," Debra said, wagging a finger at him.

Dan took another long sip of water to avoid a coughing relapse. "I don't know what you mean."

He considered his plate, trying to decide what he could eat that wouldn't choke him when Debra said something else shocking. He had the feeling she was bent on doing that for the rest of the meal.

When she remained silent for longer than he expected, he glanced up to see her watching him closely. There was no amusement on her face. No sign of her teasing. Rather, he found a mixture of curiosity and sadness.

"You know, Mom wanted you to go on. Perhaps even get married again."

Dan was glad he didn't have anything in his mouth. He looked everywhere but at his daughter. "How's that salad of yours? The cooks really know their stuff here, don't they?"

He felt Debra's hand on his and looked into her face to find her smiling. "You're doing it again."

"Doing what?"

"Changing the subject when it comes to Mom."

There was no point denying it. She was right.

"Then again, this really isn't about Mom, is it?" she asked. "This is about you. And Natalie."

Dan didn't quite know what to say. If someone had told him a week ago that he would be sitting here talking about his love life with his daughter, he would have called him a liar.

Now that it was happening, he didn't know quite what to do.

"She didn't say anything when I saw her at the gym yesterday," Debra said. "But she didn't have to. Like you, there's something…different about her."

"Different good, or different bad?"

His daughter paused thoughtfully. "Just different. The good or bad part…I guess that's up to the two of you."

Dan nodded, finally giving up on eating, and pushing his plate away. "You know I loved your mother, Deb…."

"Yes, I do know. If only because sometimes I envied that love."

For a moment Dan considered her. She smiled at him encouragingly. "So it wouldn't bother you, you know, if something happened between the lady doc and me?"

Her smile widened. "Bother me? Are you kidding? I've been trying to match the two of you up for three months."

Dan jerked back as if he'd just taken a physical blow.

"You didn't really think I hounded you about going to your appointments because I was worried about you, did you?" She made a face. "Okay, I *was* really worried about you. But I was also hoping that you and Natalie would hit it off."

"Hit it off" seemed to fall so far short of the mark that Dan averted his gaze. There was no way his daughter could know what he was thinking, but there was no sense in taking chances.

"And?" Debra asked. "What really did happen on that island?"

Dan grinned at her. "Well, I think that's something that's going to have to remain a mystery, darling daughter. Because my mama taught me that a true gentleman never kisses and tells...."

She gave a small squeal of approval. "Trust me, the kissing part is all I needed to know."

NATALIE TOOK the broiled red potatoes and onions from the oven and put them on the stovetop, then checked the fresh green beans steaming in the double boiler. She wiped her hands on a towel and leaned against the counter, picking up her half-full wineglass. It wasn't all that long ago when she would have been satisfied with preparing a simple meal for herself. When she would look around her town house in the foothills of Courage Bay and feel a sense of accomplishment. The carefully chosen tapestry-covered furniture, paintings by local artist Lucy Arnold, her wine collection—all these things usually brought her a measure of comfort.

Now she regarded them as many things she didn't need.

She slowly sipped the merlot and walked around the first floor of the three-story town house. Too big. Stuffed full of too many possessions. She caught herself rubbing the sleeve of her silk blouse, and looked down at the rich material, almost surprised to find herself wearing it. Instead of the blouse, the light wool slacks and low-heeled shoes she'd dressed in for work that day, she'd expected to see the simple cotton T-shirt and borrowed khaki pants she'd worn on S-hamala Island.

Empty. That's how the house felt. Only she hadn't realized it until just then. That's likely why she spent so much time cramming it with objects, trying to fill a void that couldn't be filled with material things.

She stepped to the stereo and flipped through the CDs, but nothing caught her attention. Her favorite singers held little appeal tonight. She stared at the tuner. She usually never listened to the radio, but almost without realizing what she was doing, she pushed the power button, then flipped through the stations until the brassy sound of big band music reverberated through the large, airy rooms. She smiled and tucked her glass against her chest.

Ever since returning from the island, she'd felt…peculiar. As if she'd been knocked out of her groove and couldn't find her way back into it. The grief that had plagued her was a dull ache now instead of a sharp, piercing sensation. She missed Charles. Probably always would. Although every now and again, she wondered if it was the man she missed so much, or the plans they'd once made.

She tried to imagine Charles with her now. If he'd survived his heart attack, they would have married, and he would be part of the household. They had planned to move into her house following the wedding, since his apartment was older and on the opposite side of town, farther from both their jobs.

Natalie frowned. Was that why they'd chosen her town house? Not because they liked the style or the spectacular view, but because it was centrally located?

She placed her wineglass on top of the stereo cabinet and rubbed her arms, warding off a shiver. She tried not to think about how…cold she'd felt since returning to the mainland. Nothing seemed capable of warming her. Funny… She'd spent four days and three nights in damp clothing in a drafty cabin with a hole in the roof, and she couldn't remember ever feeling as cold as she did right now. But then she hadn't been alone.

Dan…

The mere thought of him sent a burst of warmth flowing through her system. His presence had filled every corner of the cabin, just as it now filled her heart.

Natalie walked down the hall toward the kitchen, the click of her heels against the polished wood floor sounding abnormally loud. She hadn't heard from Dan since they'd shared the solemn boat ride back to the mainland together. Not that she'd expected to. Circumstances were unfolding exactly as she'd anticipated they would. She had gone back to her life, and he to his.

After checking the brisket, she closed the oven door, wondering if his life felt as different as hers did.

She glanced around the yellow-and-white kitchen with its stainless steel appliances and gleaming tiles. Would Dan like it here? What did his place look like? He might be able to heat up a mean can of soup and open MREs, but did he know how to cook? Did he do dishes?

It bothered her that she didn't even know what his favorite color was. She'd been as intimate as a woman could be with a man—twice—and she didn't know the simplest things about him.

Which was why, perhaps, it was better just to leave what had happened on the island in the past. Where could they possibly go from there? Backtrack and start going out to dinner? Dating?

But you know more important things than his favorite color, a little voice whispered to her.

And she did. She knew how he felt about his late wife. She knew how gentle he was when he touched her. How hurt he'd been when he'd lost Spike, and that he didn't complain about his arm falling asleep when she spent all night on top of it.

Natalie knew she loved the feel of his hands against her body, reveled in his kiss and slept so soundly in his arms that she'd forgotten there was a storm raging around them and a dangerous fugitive lurking outside.

And somewhere down the line, she'd forgotten herself.

Natalie idly tucked a lock of hair behind her ear— her carefully straightened hair. That wasn't right; she hadn't forgotten herself. Dan had awakened in her a new sense of self, unwittingly uncovered another dimension. One that was more down-to-earth, tuned in to simple pleasures.

And without him in the picture, her new self didn't fit in with the old one.

She stepped to the telephone on the wall and lifted the receiver, staring at the number pad for a long time without dialing. All she'd have to do was call 411 to get both his home and work numbers. In less than a minute she could be talking to him, asking what his favorite color was. Asking him if he thought at all about what had happened on the island. She could be inviting him to dinner and finding out if he liked brisket.

Slowly she replaced the receiver in its cradle, leaving her hand there for a long moment before finally drawing it away. When it came right down to it, she couldn't call him. It was more than fear of his rejecting her. She'd gotten used to his mood swings on the island and knew her chances of getting a cool reception were fifty-fifty. The reason she was hesitant to reach out was that if he had wreaked so many changes in her life during their few short days stranded together, what would he do now?

"I want to marry you because we share so much in common...."

Those had been Charles's words when he'd proposed to her and she'd asked him why he thought they should get married.

She and Dan had nothing in common. He'd hate gallery openings and the theater. He'd probably sit on the edge of her couch as if afraid he might get it dirty. She'd offer wine and he would ask for beer. She'd want to order in sushi and he'd want homemade meat loaf.

None of that had mattered on the island, where they were forced to scrape by with the bare necessities. But here...

The alarm on the stove buzzed, indicating her brisket was done. She slid her hand into an oven mitt and removed the dish just as the phone rang.

Natalie's heart skipped a beat.

She stood for long moments staring at the phone.

Was it him?

She reached for the receiver with her mitt-covered hand, fumbled to remove it, then pressed the answer button.

"Hello?"

"Aunt Natalie!"

Not Dan.

It was her niece, Stacy. A voice equally welcome. Almost…

CHAPTER SEVENTEEN

THE FOLLOWING MORNING, Dan knelt before the marble memorial bearing Eleanor's name and replaced the wilting daisies in the vase in front of it with a fresh bunch. The sun was rising over Courage Bay Mountain behind him, and the Pacific stretched in front, a gentle breeze all but blowing away the memory of the severe storms that had battered the coast only a few days earlier.

Dan stood up and slid his hands into his jeans pockets, his wedding ring snagging on the stitched edging. He stood staring at the headstone he'd chosen because he thought his wife would have liked it. On the right side of the pale rose marble was an oval picture of the three of them, Ellie, Dan and Debra, and above Ellie's name was etched the phrase Loving Wife and Mother. He stared at these words, waiting for the connection to hit him. That strong sense of belonging to something bigger than him—his marriage.

The wind picked up, blowing against him from behind, rustling the daisies and making him shudder slightly. He felt nothing but a gentle sense of loss. Warm memories and sad goodbyes. Laughter and heartbreak. Hope.

Hope?

He hadn't felt the emotion for so long he'd almost forgotten what it was like. After losing Ellie, he'd never expected to feel hope again. To look out across the lush coastal landscape with a quiet anticipation that the sun would rise and set, the tides would ebb and flow, the sea lions would honk and the world would continue to turn.

To look forward to tomorrow and hope it would be even better than today.

He'd spent so long with one foot rooted in the past that he hadn't dared look very far ahead. Then Natalie had held out her arms to him, coaxing him to free himself, to free his heart.

Eleanor...

He knelt down again, resting his forearms against his thighs. There was a time when he'd thought himself incapable of loving anyone but her.

Then again, perhaps it was loving her that had paved the way for him to love again.

To love Natalie.

As he reached out to touch his fingertips to the cool marble, his wedding band caught the golden light of the sunrise and reflected it. He stared down at the band for a long time, the last visual proof, aside from Debra, of his connection to Ellie.

He called forth an image of his wife and was immediately rewarded with one of her smiling at him.

Right on the heels of that was an image of Natalie's face just as he'd kissed her for the last time before leaving the island.

Dan closed his eyes and touched the gold band that had been on his finger for so long he didn't know if he could get it off. He gave an experimental tug and found it easily slid free.

He stared down at the wedding band, his heart pounding in his chest. Something etched inside caught his attention, so he lifted it closer and squinted to read the words. He'd forgotten that he and Eleanor had had their rings engraved when they'd picked them out.

Love you forever, Ellie.

Dan's throat grew tight. In that moment, he knew those words to be the truth. He also knew that he would love Ellie forever. Nothing would change that. He didn't need a ring to remember her.

But it didn't mean he couldn't go on to love another.

Love Natalie.

He knelt in front of the headstone again and fastened the ring to the ribbon tied around the daisies. Then he kissed his fingertips and pressed them against his late wife's name.

"Love you forever…."

What seemed like a long time later, Dan rose to his feet and left the cemetery, filled with an emotion he'd thought he would never feel again: Joy.

NATALIE HELD OUT a variety of lollipops for little Jenny Barnard to choose from. The girl's superficial facial burn was healing nicely. It seemed the talk they'd had during her last appointment had worked. Jenny had allowed her mother to change her dressings and apply the ointment without argument.

The girl chose a grape sucker.

"I wish all my patients did such a good job of looking after their burns as you and your mom are doing," Natalie said, lightly chucking Jenny under her chin.

Both mother and daughter smiled, and Natalie felt a warm rush of pleasure.

As she watched her young patient walk off down the hall, her hand in her mother's, Natalie clutched the medical chart to her chest, the warm feeling fading.

It had been three days since she'd returned from the island. Anyone would need time to adjust after such an ordeal. But while her patients' wounds were visible on the outside, her own weren't discernable to the human eye. No, only she knew what lurked inside her heart, and she wasn't ready to show anyone just yet. It was all too fresh, too new. She needed time to adjust before she decided on an action plan.

And a plan of action was just what she would need in order to win over Dan Egan's mind. Natalie was pretty sure she had made significant headway into his heart.

She slid Jenny's chart into the outgoing slot and glanced at the file in the incoming one. "Manuela? I don't understand. I thought there were no more patients today."

Her assistant was tidying up her desk and taking her purse out of her bottom drawer, obviously calling it a day. "We had a drop-in I thought you should see."

"A drop-in?" She never got drop-ins. She opened the file, only to find it empty. "There's nothing in here."

Manuela was walking down the hall, waving goodbye. "Examining room three."

Natalie opened her mouth to stop her from leaving, but her feisty assistant was already stepping into an open elevator, out of earshot.

Well, that's odd.

Walking over to Manuela's desk, Natalie checked to see if the file documents had somehow fallen out. But there was nothing on the spotless desk. A new patient? Possibly. But if that were the case, why hadn't Manuela put new patient forms inside the file? It wasn't like her.

"Hey, sis."

She looked up to see her younger brother, Alec, approaching.

He kissed her lightly on the cheek, then leaned back and frowned at her. "You okay? You're looking a little pale around the edges."

Natalie considered him. "Mmm. I think so. A long day, that's all."

Alec studied her closely, his hazel eyes intense. "Are you sure that's all it is?"

She nodded and averted her gaze for fear of what he might see if he looked too closely.

Although he seemed unconvinced, Alec apparently decided to concede the point. "Okay. I just dropped by to see if you wanted to pick up a bite for dinner with me. Janice is taking the kids Christmas shopping and I'm flying solo tonight."

Dinner. Although she'd only had a yogurt cup for lunch, she wasn't hungry in the least. "I, um, can't. I still have a patient to see."

Alec looked at his watch. "This late?"

She nodded. "So it would appear."

How Alec had changed these past few months, Natalie noted with a slight smile. Before Janice had come into his life, he wouldn't have noticed if anyone was working late, since he'd practically lived at the hospital himself.

"Okay, then," he said. "If you change your mind, I'll be at the CB Bar and Grill."

"Okay," she said, watching him walk down the hall toward the elevator.

Natalie rubbed her forehead, then gathered the necessary patient forms from the cabinet behind Manuela's desk. Checking her pocket for a pen, she stepped toward examining room three and opened the door.

Dan.

"What on earth are you doing here?" Natalie asked, putting the file on the counter, a flush warming her skin.

He gave her what had to be his most toe-curling grin. "I hear it said that you're the best burn specialist around."

Natalie smiled. "Helps when you're the only one. In Courage Bay, that is."

Despite her modest words, what he'd said had pleased her enormously.

For long moments, neither of them said anything, merely gazed at each other in a way that thickened Natalie's blood and made her knees feel as substantial as cotton balls.

"So," she murmured, "has Debra been at you again to make an appointment?"

Dan cleared his throat. "Actually, no. After everything that happened, she seems to have forgotten about hounding me about the burn."

"But you haven't forgotten—about the burn, that is."

He shook his head. "It's been bothering me ever since we got back. Along with other things."

Suddenly Natalie found it difficult to breathe. So what else had been bothering him since their return?

Somehow she managed to convince her legs to co-operate, and went to stand behind the examining table. "Do you want to take off your shirt, or would you like me to do it?"

"Depends on what you have in mind."

Natalie was glad he couldn't see her smile. "Are you coming on to your doctor, Chief Egan?"

"Well, I guess that all depends on what my doctor thinks of that." He pulled off his shirt, tousling his hair in the process and giving her free rein over his rock-hard torso.

She swallowed. How could she have forgotten how wonderfully toned he was? Burn aside, he had the body of a man half his age. And she knew that he also had the stamina.

Her face heated as she turned the examining light on his burn, and she forced her mind back to the matter at hand.

The scar tissue looked angry and painful. "I hate to tell you this, but considering our...personal involvement, I think it's best I refer you to a specialist at UCLA Med Center."

He turned his head to look at her.

"You're going to need surgery to excise the worst of this scar tissue, Dan. Extensive skin grafts. Then lots of rehab."

He didn't say anything.

She lightly probed the scar. "Do you want me to schedule an appointment for you?"

"No, I want you...."

Natalie rounded the exam table so she could look into his face. As she did so, she brushed his left hand. She looked down to find that his wedding band was gone. In its place was a white line that contrasted sharply with his tanned skin.

The absence of the ring made her heart pound against her rib cage.

"What I meant to say is I want you to do it," he murmured, clearing his throat again.

She told him he could put his shirt back on. "Okay. But I'm going to have to ask you to sign special forms."

"Will it take long? The surgery, I mean?"

"The surgery itself shouldn't be so bad. But unfortunately the whole process, and the recuperation period, will take some time."

He nodded solemnly.

Natalie couldn't help but admire him. And also question if he was the same man she had practically had to chase down last week for a simple follow-up exam. Of course, his reluctance could have had something to do with his knowing there was a serious problem with the burn. But that still didn't explain his complete reversal in his decision to seek her out, to have the wound treated.

Was he also feeling that something had changed during their brief time on the island?

He pulled his shirt back on and smoothed it over his flat abs. "So…I guess that's that then."

She nodded and collected her chart from the counter, doing something, anything, other than look at him. "That's that. I'll be in contact with a time and date for the surgery."

He pushed himself off the table, towering over her in a way that took her breath away.

Somehow she'd forgotten how big he was. How solid. And how damn sexy.

When he hesitated in front of her, Natalie stared at the pattern on his shirt, not sure what to do.

He made the decision for her by bending down and kissing her.

Every muscle in Natalie's body liquefied as she leaned into him. If she'd had any doubts that what had passed between them on the island had been a temporary distraction, they were completely erased. During those few precious days, she had fallen in love with Dan Egan, pigheadedness and alpha male tendencies included.

Dan pulled away, his grin tugging at something inside her chest.

"Well, goodbye then," he said quietly.

"Um, yes. Goodbye."

Natalie felt as if she was trembling straight down

to her sensible shoes as she watched him leave the room. She stood like that for long moments, her palms damp against the chart, her breathing ragged.

What had that been about? Had he been as anxious as she was to prove something existed between them beyond what their enforced isolation had created? If so, what did he think?

Shaking her head to clear it, she turned to check the room before leaving.

A small box was sitting on the table, right where Dan had been seated moments before.

Natalie looked toward the closed door, then back at the box.

An early Christmas present?

Or had Dan accidentally left it behind?

She slowly advanced, her gaze glued to the red bow. Maybe he'd bought something for Debra before he'd come here, and had forgotten to take it with him.

Natalie tried to convince herself of that even as she noticed how precisely the box had been placed on the table. And how neatly her name was written on the small tag.

She pressed the chart harder against her chest with one hand and slowly reached out with the other to pick up the box, which she saw now was for jewelry. Her fingers were trembling so violently she nearly dropped it. Anchoring it against her other hand, she snapped the box open.

And stared at the most perfect golden sapphire she'd ever seen.

Behind her, Dan quietly cleared his throat. "I didn't know if you'd prefer a diamond. At the time, I thought the sapphire matched your eyes, and that's why I chose it. Hell, I didn't even know sapphires came in that color. But if you'd rather have a diamond…"

Still holding the box, Natalie turned to look at him. He stood leaning against the doorjamb. She hadn't even heard the door open.

"I…I don't understand," Natalie whispered, unable to blink, afraid to breathe.

Dan slid his hands into his pockets, staring at his shoes. "You don't have to answer me now. Hell, we don't have to set a date for anytime soon…"

"Answer? Date?" The box in her hands snapped closed. "Dan, you haven't asked me anything."

He looked up at her, his grin making her blood rush through her veins. "You're right, I haven't, have I?"

She shook her head and resisted the urge to back up as he approached.

Too fast, a small voice whispered.

She'd spent the past three days wondering if Dan even recalled their time together on S-hamala Island, and now he was…proposing to her?

As impossible as it seemed, that's exactly what he was doing.

She gasped when he dropped to one knee in front of her. He glanced around and frowned. "I should be doing this somewhere nicer."

Natalie thought she might faint. "I think you should just do it."

He grinned, took the chart from her hands and tossed it on the examining table, then warmly grasped her fingers, which still held the ring box.

"You're right. Of course. I'm coming to see you're right about a lot of things."

Natalie's heart pounded so hard she thought it might break through the wall of her chest. "Dan..."

"Oh, yeah. Right." His gaze was intense as he stared straight up at her. "What I was going to ask, what I've been meaning to say is..."

Her mouth went dry.

"Will you do me the honor of being my wife, Dr. Natalie Giroux?"

There they were. The words she'd suspected he was going to say.

And she couldn't seem to work a response out of her tight throat.

She couldn't seem to work a response from her shell-shocked mind.

So she relied on what had seen her through so many years, especially the past year after losing Charles—her common sense.

"Get up from the floor before you catch a cold."

Dan blinked at her as if she'd just spoken a foreign language.

"That's your answer?"

She searched his all too handsome, too confused face. "I don't know what to say, Dan." She narrowed her eyes, first shaking her head, then nodding. "Don't you think this is all a little…fast?"

He finally rose to stand before her. Natalie swallowed hard.

"I know this probably wasn't the brightest idea," he said. "You know, leaving the ring on the examining table, proposing to you here and all. But the truth is…"

She searched his eyes.

"The truth is you intimidate the hell out of me, Doc."

Natalie tried to make sense out of what he was saying. "I…intimidate…you."

He nodded. "You forgot 'hell.' You intimidate the hell out of me."

Natalie smiled. "That's why you left the ring on the table."

He nodded again, looking adorably like a teenager asking a girl out on their first date.

Only he wasn't asking her out for one night. He was asking her to spend the rest of her life with him.

"Dan…" she said, trying to find words to match her feelings, and coming up woefully short.

"Wait. Don't say anything yet." He shifted from foot to foot. "I have something to tell you first."

"More than the…intimidation thing?"

He grinned. "Yes."

"All right…"

Still, he remained silent for a long time before he finally spoke. "In the past couple years, I'd come to believe my life was over."

Natalie nodded in understanding. "After Ellie died."

"No."

She raised her eyebrows.

"I mean, yes, losing Ellie had something to do with it. A lot to do with it. But it was more than that. I'd look at Spike, see how he was getting older, then I'd look at myself in the mirror and see those same signs. I was promoted to chief when I would much rather have remained on the front line. It seemed everywhere I turned, everywhere I went, I was reminded that I wasn't…young anymore."

Natalie didn't know what to say.

"And then you appeared," he said.

The bottom seemed to fall out of her stomach, as if she was on a roller-coaster ride. Only this wasn't a ride that would stop in a few minutes. A ride she could get off. This was her life.

"Doc, you…well, you made me take a closer look at myself. Made me see that my life was far from over. You made me realize that instead of waiting for the end to come, I should look at each day as one more to be filled with love. With happiness."

Emotion clogged Natalie's throat. "I did all that?"

He curved his fingers around the side of her neck. "Oh, yes. And much more." His gaze dropped to her mouth. Natalie licked her lips, readying herself for his kiss. Then he was looking into her eyes again. "I love you, Doc. It's as simple and as complicated as that."

A small sound escaped her.

"I didn't think it was possible. You know, for me to love anyone again. But, oh, how you proved me wrong. And I'm not the kind of guy to wait around. Once I know something, I know it. Why waste any more time than I already have?"

Natalie's fingers tightened around the ring box. "But we have nothing in common."

She'd whispered the words, but felt as if she'd used a bullhorn to broadcast them.

Dan blinked at her. Then he grinned so widely he took her breath away. Slowly he leaned down to brush his lips against hers.

The floor seemed to shift under Natalie's feet. Her heart beat so hard she thought she could hear it. She wanted this man—with everything inside her.

Dan pulled away and smiled deep into her eyes. "Do you like basketball?"

She shook her head.

"How about baseball?"

She thought about it a moment. "I like baseball."

She realized she could spend an eternity staring into his warm eyes.

"So we start there, then," he said. "Find the things we do share in common. And begin building from them." There was a teasing glint in his eyes. "There have to be other things we can agree on. Food. Friends. And while I haven't been good with compromise before now, I'm willing to try. You know, if you are."

As Natalie looked at him, basked in the warmth of his love, she couldn't imagine living another day of her life without him in it.

"Baseball," she repeated.

He grinned. "Uh-huh."

She found herself grinning back. "I think I can do that."

She more than knew she could do that. Even if she were a vegetarian and he a meat lover, if his favorite color was black and hers was white, her love for him was so all-consuming, so empowering, that together they would not only find common ground, they would find a way to live happily together.

And he was right about the time aspect. If the past year had taught her anything, it was that life was too fleeting. She needed to learn how to grasp hold of it tightly with both hands and listen to her heart as much, if not more, as she listened to her head.

And she had the feeling that Dan would help her do that.

"I love you," Natalie whispered, closing her eyes and resting her forehead against his chin, emotion nearly overwhelming her. "God, how I love you."

Dan gathered her against his chest, holding her so tightly she nearly couldn't breathe.

Natalie laughed softly and looked up at him. "And I can think of nothing I'd like more than to go to a baseball game with you. You know, when the season starts up again."

His hold on her relaxed as he searched her face.

She smiled. "Oh…and become your wife…."

* * * * *

Ordinary people. Extraordinary circumstances.
Meet a new generation of heroes—
the men and women of Courage Bay Emergency
Services.
CODE RED
A new Harlequin continuity series continues
December 2004 with
BLOWN AWAY
by Muriel Jensen

Being rescued by gorgeous K-9 Officer Cole
Winslow is a fantasy come true for single mom Kara
Abbott—especially when Cole continues to be there
for her *and* her eight-year-old son. Yet Kara senses
she wants more from Cole than he's willing to give.
And Cole *is* holding back—but not for the reasons
she thinks. Now it's Kara's turn to be there for Cole,
and rescue *him*…from the grip of his past.

Here's a preview.

CHAPTER ONE

KARA WAS TERRIFIED. On the one hand, these men wanted to get her down. But as far as she could tell, there was no way to do that without running a great risk of falling. She loved flight, but she hated falling. Gliding on the wind was one thing, falling like an anvil quite another.

"We're all connected now, Kara," the cop said with that confident tone. She didn't trust confidence anymore. Danny had always been so sure of everything, certain the next scheme was going to work, the next investment, the next purchase. But all those great ideas did was get them into deeper trouble. "You're going to come right down here with me."

"Guys, I don't know…"

"Your little boy's waiting," the cop said.

He'd mentioned her son earlier, but this time terror leaped inside her. "How do you know about him?" she asked, then screamed as the branch she hung from bounced.

"Your boss, Frank, told me," the cop said. "How we doing, Gehlen?"

"Get ready," Gehlen replied. "I'm going to cut."

Oh, dear God! Taylor! What would happen to him if she didn't come home? Would he end up in foster care? Her parents were gone, she had no siblings, no true friendships to speak of, she worked all the time to provide for Taylor and spent what free time she had with him.

"Here we go, Kara!" Gehlen said.

The chaos that thoughts of Taylor created in her mind seemed to extend beyond her. The world spun and drove wildly around her, making her feel panicky and dizzy.

"It's going to work, Kara!" she heard the cop shout up at her.

"Are you sure?" she shouted desperately.

"I'm sure!"

"Heads up, Cole!" Gehlen shouted, and Kara felt a small tug that set her free. Suddenly she was racing toward death at a speed that made her eyes tear and the wind sing in her ears.

The rich green around her flew by. She knew it! They'd done something wrong and she was going to plummet to the bottom. The thread by which her life had been hanging for years had finally snapped.

She'd known it would happen someday. She'd just hoped Taylor would be working in a law firm by then, or set up in a dental practice, or working for NASA. Oh, Taylor.

Then, before she could prepare for it, she slammed into the waiting arms of Sergeant Winslow like a lover.

Terror and the real conviction that this could not possibly end well, that his confidence had been as faulty as Danny's was and they were both going to tumble headlong to their deaths, made her cling to him, eyes tightly shut, teeth gritted, waiting for the inevitable.

It didn't happen. The harness from which he was suspended swung in a wide arc. She screamed and held on to him with every ounce of energy she had, arms clutching his broad back, one leg curled around his. He held her to him with considerable strength and she heard the clink of a hook as he disconnected her from one rope and tied her to him.

"Are you okay?" he asked.

"Yes," she whispered, eyes still closed, hands still clinging.

"Cole!" she heard Gehlen shout.

"We're fine!" Cole called back. "She's okay. Just a little shaken."

A little? She wanted to laugh out loud.

And when her senses finally overpowered her emotions, she began to be aware of the body to which she clung. It was like rock, or one of the trees all around them—made from nature's strongest stuff.

God, it felt good to be held. It didn't matter that there was nothing remotely sexual about it. Her life was now centered on her son and simple survival, anyway. But it was wonderful to let someone else be in charge, if only for the time it took to get down to the ground. And this man's shoulders felt as though he could carry her all the way.

CODE RED

Ordinary People. Extraordinary Circumstances.

If you've enjoyed getting to know the men and women of California's Courage Bay Emergency Services team, Harlequin Books invites you to return to Courage Bay!

Just collect six (6) proofs of purchase from the back of six (6) different CODE RED titles and receive four (4) free CODE RED books that are not currently available in retail outlets!

Just complete the order form and send it, along with six (6) proofs of purchase from six (6) different CODE RED titles, to: CODE RED, P.O. Box 9047, Buffalo, NY 14269-9047, or P.O. Box 613, Fort Erie, Ontario L2A 5X3. (Cost of $1.50 for shipping and handling applies.)

Name (PLEASE PRINT)

Address   Apt. #

City   State/Prov.   Zip/Postal Code

093 KKA DXH7

When you return six proofs of purchase, you will receive the following titles:
RIDING THE STORM by Julie Miller   **TURBULENCE** by Jessica Matthews
WASHED AWAY by Carol Marinelli   **HARD RAIN** by Darlene Scalera

To receive your free CODE RED books (retail value $19.96), complete the above form. Mail it to us with six proofs of purchase, one of which can be found in the right-hand corner of this page. Requests must be received no later than October 31, 2005. Your set of four CODE RED books costs you only $1.50 shipping and handling. N.Y. state residents must add applicable sales tax on shipping and handling charge. Please allow 6–8 weeks for receipt of order. Offer good in Canada and U.S. only. Offer good while quantities last.

When you respond to this offer, we will also send you *Inside Romance*, a free quarterly publication, highlighting upcoming releases and promotions from Harlequin and Silhouette Books.

❑ If you do not wish to receive this free publication, please check here.

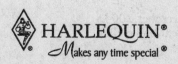

HARLEQUIN®
Makes any time special®

CODE RED
ONE PROOF OF PURCHASE
CRPOP3

The men and women of California's
Courage Bay Emergency Services team
must face any emergency...even the
ones that are no accident!

Coming in December...

B L O W N
A W A Y

by

MURIEL
JENSEN

Being rescued by gorgeous K-9 Officer
Cole Winslow is a fantasy come true for
single mom Kara Abbott. But, despite
their mutual attraction, Kara senses
Cole is holding back. Now it's Kara's
turn to rescue Cole—from the grip
of his past.

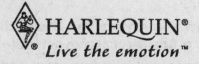

If you enjoyed what you just read,
then we've got an offer you can't resist!

Take 2 bestselling novels FREE!
Plus get a FREE surprise gift!

Clip this page and mail it to MIRA®

IN U.S.A.
3010 Walden Ave.
P.O. Box 1867
Buffalo, N.Y. 14240-1867

IN CANADA
P.O. Box 609
Fort Erie, Ontario
L2A 5X3

YES! Please send me 2 free MIRA® novels and my free surprise gift. After receiving them, if I don't wish to receive anymore, I can return the shipping statement marked cancel. If I don't cancel, I will receive 4 brand-new novels every month, before they're available in stores! In the U.S.A., bill me at the bargain price of $4.99 plus 25¢ shipping and handling per book and applicable sales tax, if any*. In Canada, bill me at the bargain price of $5.49 plus 25¢ shipping and handling per book and applicable taxes**. That's the complete price and a savings of over 20% off the cover prices—what a great deal! I understand that accepting the 2 free books and gift places me under no obligation ever to buy any books. I can always return a shipment and cancel at any time. Even if I never buy another The Best of the Best™ book, the 2 free books and gift are mine to keep forever.

185 MDN DZ7J
385 MDN DZ7K

Name	(PLEASE PRINT)	
Address	Apt.#	
City	State/Prov.	Zip/Postal Code

Not valid to current The Best of the Best™, Mira®,
suspense and romance subscribers.

Want to try two free books from another series?
Call 1-800-873-8635 or visit www.morefreebooks.com.

* Terms and prices subject to change without notice. Sales tax applicable in N.Y.
** Canadian residents will be charged applicable provincial taxes and GST.
   All orders subject to approval. Offer limited to one per household.
® and ™are registered trademarks owned and used by the trademark owner or its licensee.

BOB04R   ©2004 Harlequin Enterprises Limited

eHARLEQUIN.com

The Ultimate Destination for Women's Fiction

The eHarlequin.com online community is *the* place to share opinions, thoughts and feelings!

- Joining the community is easy, fun and **FREE!**

- Connect with **other romance fans** on our message boards.

- Meet your **favorite authors** without leaving home!

- **Share opinions** on books, movies, celebrities…and *more!*

Here's what our members say:

"I love the friendly and helpful atmosphere filled with support and humor."
—Texanna (eHarlequin.com member)

"Is this the place for me, or what? There is nothing I love more than 'talking' books, especially with fellow readers who are reading the same ones I am."
—Jo Ann (eHarlequin.com member)

Join today by visiting
www.eHarlequin.com!